M000165469

If he could only see her...

THE MAN WITH THE scar placed a foot on one of the crates, lit a cigarette and leaned forward, casually resting an elbow on his knee. He took a deep drag off his cigarette and then exhaled slowly.

"You've made a mistake," Simon said. "We're not whomever you think we are."

"No?"

"Let us go and we promise not to say anything about this," Elizabeth said.

Simon heard the defiance and the fear in her voice. The man with the scar just laughed. Simon knew what that laughter meant. He closed his eyes and tried to calm himself. His only weapon was his mind. Maybe he could negotiate with them. He seemed to be their target.

"Let her go. You can keep me," Simon said. He was desperate to find some way, any way to get Elizabeth out of there. "I'll do whatever you ask, if you let her go..."

The Out of Time Series
by Monique Martin

Out of Time

When the Walls Fell

Fragments

Please check Monique's website,
http://moniquemartin.weebly.com/
for news of new and upcoming books!

MONIQUE MARTIN

Fragments

Out of Time Series
Book 3

Copyright Notice

This book is a work of fiction. Names, characters, places and incidents either are the product of the author's imagination or are used fictitiously. Any resemblance to actual persons, living or dead, is entirely coincidental.

Copyright © 2012 Monique Martin

All rights reserved. No part of this publication may be reproduced or transmitted in any form or by any means, electronic or mechanical, without written permission.

Cover Photo: Karen Wunderman
Cover Layout: TERyvisions

ISBN 10: 0984660739
ISBN 13: 978-0-9846607-3-5

For more information, please contact
writtenbymonique@gmail.com
Or visit: www.moniquemartin.weebly.com

First Paperback Edition

ACKNOWLEDGEMENTS

THIS BOOK WOULD NOT have been possible without the help and support of many people: Robin, who I can't thank enough and who makes writing fun; Dad and Anne; Mom and George; Eddie and Carole; Michael; Melissa; Mel; JM; Vicki and all the wonderful people who sent notes of encouragement along the way.

I'd also like to thank the thousands of people who help preserve the past through books, websites, museums and sheer will.

Fragments

Monique Martin

CHAPTER ONE

"**R**EMORSELESS. MALEVOLENT. PUTRESCENT. THIS creature will feed on your fear like scavengers sucking marrow from a bone."

Elizabeth watched Simon pace restlessly at the front of the lecture hall. The tension was palpable in every word, in every stride he took across the auditorium floor. His cut-glass British accent was sharp, but his deep baritone voice was deceptively gentle and subtly magnetic. She'd always thought half the students in his class came just to hear him speak.

"Far worse than the Harpy of Greek mythology, this harridan will try to poison you," he said before stopping to grip the edges of the lectern and lean forward. Elizabeth felt herself mirroring his movement and edged forward in her seat.

Simon's eyes fixed on hers and the amber flecks in his deep green eyes sparked with intensity. "Mark my words," he continued, "You will be eaten alive."

Elizabeth frowned. "I'm sure your Aunt isn't that bad, Simon."

"You haven't met her yet."

Elizabeth's laugh echoed through the empty lecture hall. Hours ago, the last student from Simon's Introduction to Occult Studies

1

class had fled the university eager to get a head start on Spring Break. She was anxious to do the same and would have if Simon hadn't felt compelled to warn her about his family. Again. She gathered her bag, lighter now that the final papers had all been graded, and joined him near the podium. "It's been ten years since you've seen them. Maybe they've mellowed."

Simon shook his head. "Scotch and red wine mellow, but not my relatives, I'm afraid."

Elizabeth had endured Simon's warnings for the last few weeks, which was odd since the whole vacation to England idea had been his. At first she'd thought he was just being dramatic, but now with zero hour fast approaching, she wasn't so sure.

"Last chance to back out," Simon said.

Her stomach tightened a little bit more, but she waved a dismissive hand. "It'll be fine."

"I still think we should go straight to my grandfather's house in Hastings."

"And miss seeing Grey Hall, birthplace of the great Simon Cross?" Elizabeth still couldn't wrap her mind around the fact that Simon was actually a baronet and had a big old country estate to prove it.

"One night," Simon said, "and even that will sorely test the levels of my patience."

"You have levels?"

"Amusing."

Elizabeth tipped her head back and put on her best Cockney accent. "You must be barmy, guv'nah."

"You promised. "

"Right ho!"

"Elizabeth."

"That was the last time," she said and sealed her promise with a kiss on his cheek. "I swear."

Simon didn't look convinced.

"Pip...pip?"

Simon tried to frown, but couldn't quite manage it. Although, the smile that touched the corners of his eyes didn't last long either.

"I've got it out of my system now. Don't worry," she said. "I won't embarrass you."

Simon's eyes clouded over. "That, I can assure you, is not what I'm worried about."

"I had my shots," she said with a grin that quickly fell. "I don't actually need shots, do I?"

Simon chuckled. "No."

"Well, it's my first time out of the country, if you don't count the time I got lost in Juarez, which you shouldn't because I didn't even know I was in Mexico until I wasn't anymore."

"That doesn't make any sense at all."

"I know," Elizabeth said as she slipped her arm through his. "Now, come on, I still have packing to do."

"Still?"

"And I need to stop at the mall."

"God help me."

Being an experienced time traveler somehow didn't prepare Elizabeth for actual travel travel. Not that it was bad. In fact, it was nice, very nice. When the town car pulled up in front of Simon's house, she should have known that this trip wasn't going to be like the last time she'd traveled by plane. Then, she'd taken a Southwest flight from Santa Barbara to Lubbock and sat squished between a young man wearing half a bottle of Axe Body Spray and a businessman with an unfortunate glandular problem. This time, she wasn't flying cattle class. Heck, they weren't even flying first class. Leave it to Simon to find an airline with an upper class, class.

Each passenger had his or her own suite that was nicer and more spacious than her first apartment. Each suite was really a pod with privacy partitions like a work cubicle and a large reclining seat that extended into a full-length bed.

Elizabeth tried to sleep. She really did, but it was impossible. She knelt on her seat and peeked over the partition at Simon. "Whatcha doin'?"

Simon kept his eyes on his book. "Playing the banjo."

"Very funny."

Simon put his book down and looked up at her. He studied her for a long moment. He'd been doing that a lot lately. Just looking at her. At first, she'd thought it was sweet. He'd look at her, smile and then look away, almost shy, which would have been charming if it weren't so alarming. Simon was many things, but shy really wasn't one of them. Now, when he looked at her, deep, deep into her and then looked away, she had a vaguely uneasy feeling. Like something needed to be said and he just couldn't bring himself to say it.

"Why don't you have a drink and try to get some sleep?" Simon finally said. "It's a long flight."

"I know," she said, but didn't budge.

Simon pushed himself up from his seat and kissed her. "Try to sleep, darling. You'll feel better if you do."

Elizabeth chewed her bottom lip and nodded as she slid back down into her seat. She pulled the cocktail menu out of the seat-back pocket and looked for something warm and boozy.

"You could always read Aumond's last book," came Simon's voice from behind the partition. "That always does it for me."

Elizabeth snorted and rolled her eyes at the gentle barb. A cocktail was sounding better all the time. He'd finally come to understand why she'd considered a job with another professor, but he hadn't forgotten her wandering academic eye. Simon never forgot.

Elizabeth wished she could sleep; it just wasn't going to be possible. She called for the flight attendant and ordered a hot toddy. It couldn't hurt.

Aside from the excitement of seeing England and getting a glimpse into Simon's past, she was beginning to think she was a little, itty-bitty bit terrified of flying. Well, not the actual flying, but the potential crashing. It was silly. She knew the physics involved in flying, but she couldn't shake the absurd and intense feeling that her will and her will alone kept the plane in the air. Her life and the lives of everyone on board depended on her ability to stay alert and shop in the Sky Mall.

The hot toddy arrived frighteningly fast and she watched the flight attendant glide back down the aisle. She took a sip. It didn't help. There was always shopping.

Sadly, as appealing as it was to imagine being able to smoke meat in the comfort of her own kitchen or ionize her water for youthfulness and wellness, her mind kept wandering off the pages and back onto her relationship with Simon.

Their trip to 1906 San Francisco had given them both a fresh perspective. There had been a much-needed shift in their relationship that gave Elizabeth confidence in their future. They were partners now. Elizabeth's personal life had never been so full of promise. Her goals for her professional life on the other hand, weren't as clear.

She squirmed in her seat and toyed with her drink. She'd mastered her Master's and could continue on for a doctorate or… something. What that something was she didn't know, but she did know that she owed it to herself to see if she could put a few names to it. She'd always thought she'd end up teaching, like Simon, but now she wasn't so sure.

Elizabeth spent her life reading about the impossible only to find herself face to face with it. It was hard to get excited about reading someone else's theories based on bits of ancient text and third hand stories when she could be out there experiencing it firsthand.

It was all the dang watch's fault. Who knew in less than a year she'd go from grad student to time traveler? She remembered the night clearly. Time traveling for the first time wasn't exactly something a person forgot. Simon's grandfather's effects had been delivered to Simon's house and she helped him go through them. Amidst the strange artifacts was grandfather Sebastian's pocket watch. But this was no ordinary pocket watch; it was a time travel device. After they unwittingly activated the watch during an eclipse, she and Simon traveled back in time to 1929 New York City.

It seemed all of the stories Sebastian had regaled Simon with as a child, adventures in Eighteenth Century France, the American Civil War, and the rest, hadn't been imaginative stories at all. His grandfather was a member of something called the Council for Temporal Studies, a group of time traveling explorers and anthropologists.

When she and Simon had been transported to New York, she'd been a victim of circumstance, but later, when the Council for Temporal Studies had come to ask for her help, she'd gone to 1906 San Francisco willingly. Both experiences had changed her, changed the way she saw herself. Her world had gone from the narrow confines of academia to something where anything not only seemed possible, but apparently was.

Elizabeth stood at the proverbial crossroads and all the lights were green.

Elizabeth stared at the luggage carousel in a daze. The sleep she'd fought so hard against came, but never stayed. Half asleep and half awake, she leaned against Simon and watched the bags float by.

"Bugger."

"What's wrong?" she asked through a yawn.

When Simon didn't answer, she followed his gaze. Behind the ropes that separated passengers from picker-uppers stood an expressionless man with a black suit, black cap tucked under one arm and a neatly printed sign in the other that read: "Sir Simon Cross."

"I told them not to send a car," Simon grumbled through clenched teeth.

"Damned inconsiderate." Honestly, Elizabeth didn't see the problem. It clearly beat the alternatives of fighting for a cab or walking God knew how far. Of course, Simon knew his family better than she did. If sending a car and a driver to save them from public transportation was an affront, then color her affronted. Also, relieved.

"I specifically said that—" Simon started, but Elizabeth cut him off when she saw their luggage coming down the chute.

"Bag! The black one."

Simon leaned forward to look down the carousel. "They're all black."

"The one with the squiggly red ribbon."

Simon reached for the bag and heaved it off the conveyor with a grunt. "Good God."

Elizabeth checked the tag to make sure it was hers and then surveyed their luggage. "That's it. We're good. And," she said, touching his arm, "it was a nice gesture to send the car."

"It wasn't— Oh, all right. I'll pretend it was. But I'm doing this for your benefit and not theirs."

"Noted. And thank you."

It was still dark when they left the airport. Elizabeth tried to see through the tinted back windows of the car, but it was all just a blur of lights.

"There isn't much to see," Simon said. "We're outside London and Grey Hall is still over an hour's drive from here."

Elizabeth slid across the seat and rested her head on Simon's shoulder. He put his arm around her and pulled her close. "But it's *England*," she said not trying to hide the awe in her voice.

"Yes, England."

There was a longing in his voice that Elizabeth hadn't heard before. "You miss it, don't you?"

"Some things, yes. A great deal."

"Well, it is home."

"It was once."

They lapsed into a tired, but comfortable, silence as they made their way through the darkness and early morning traffic. Elizabeth snuggled into Simon's side and let her mind wander.

Simon's life in England was a bit of a mystery to her. She knew he'd moved to America shortly after Oxford and that his parents had died in a car crash about fifteen years ago. He didn't talk about them very often. Estranged in life and in death. Their passing meant that Grey Hall and the title of baronet was his. He seemed almost ashamed of both of them. If she'd been a Countess or something, she'd be counting all over the place. Or not. Class systems and titles weren't something she understood. All she knew was that for Simon, going home meant visiting ghosts of a life he'd tried too hard to forget.

Between the cloud-like suspension of the Bentley and the warmth of Simon's body, Elizabeth felt herself drifting on the edge of sleep. She tried to stay awake, but the next thing she remembered was Simon brushing back her hair and kissing her temple.

"Wake up, love. There's something I'd like to show you."

Elizabeth sat up and rubbed her eyes. It took her a moment to shake the sleep from her brain. "Are we there?" All she could see outside the window was a big, dark hedge.

"Almost." Simon got out and came around to her side of the car. "You don't mind a bit of a walk, do you?"

Elizabeth shook her head and took Simon's offered hand as she stepped out of the car. The cold morning air helped her shed the last remnants of sleep. She arched her back and stretched, admiring the enormous hedge that appeared to run the length of England.

"We'll walk from here," Simon told the driver. "Please take our bags up to the house."

"Of course, Sir Simon," acknowledged the driver, touching his cap.

After the car pulled away and disappeared down the lane, Simon took Elizabeth's hand and led her to the other side of the road.

"Sir Simon," Elizabeth said with a giggle. "That kills me."

When they reached the far side of the road, her laughter died. Her breath caught in her chest. She'd heard of breathtaking, but this was the first time she'd actually experienced it. Grey Hall was breathtaking. Beneath the still-lifting fog of morning, gentle, rolling hills spread out as far as she could see. A blanket of lush pastures with small thickets of trees and hedges created a patchwork quilt of different shades of green. A grove of trees formed a crescent around the glassy water of a pond at the base of a grand sloping lawn. At the top of the lawn was a manor house right out of "Pride and Prejudice."

"Shaka Zulu," Elizabeth muttered. "You really grew up here?" She wasn't sure if she was still dreaming or not. This couldn't be real. People, real people, didn't live like this. Mr. Darcy lived like this. Royalty lived like this. Okay, maybe Madonna lived like this, but people she knew did not.

"I spent more time at school and Grandfather's, but yes, I did. This is my favorite view. Close enough to see its charms and far enough away to be free of them."

"Was it really so bad?"

Simon smiled and shrugged. "Is any childhood as terrible or as wonderful as we remember it to be?"

Elizabeth squeezed his hand. "There must be some good memories."

"There are," he conceded and then smiled down at her. "This will be one of them."

He pulled her into his arms and kissed her with such aching gentleness that she suddenly wondered if something was wrong.

"Are you ready?" he asked, making it sound as if they were about to storm the beaches of Normandy.

"I guess so." Elizabeth nodded and Simon turned to face the road home.

"Don't say I didn't warn you."

CHAPTER TWO

EVERY MUSCLE IN SIMON'S body tensed as they neared the house. He felt like one of Pavlov's dogs. Just the sight of Grey Hall made his entire being clench in preparation for some potential battle, some cutting remark, some painful disappointment. The past hung like an albatross around his neck. Molting.

He pushed out a bracing breath. "All hope abandon, ye who enter in."

"You know, for a comedy, The Divine Comedy is not a lot of laughs," Elizabeth said.

Simon smiled and then looked at the front door. "No, and you won't find many in there either, I'm afraid."

Elizabeth took his hand. "That's all right. Better a comedy than a tragedy. At least that way, we get a happy ending, right?"

How he hoped so.

Simon opened the large doors and let Elizabeth precede him inside. The butler hurried toward them, apologized needlessly and took their coats. Simon had always appreciated the servants as a boy. He'd spent more time with most of them than he had with his own family. However, the faces had changed through the years and they were strangers to him now.

Simon guided Elizabeth further inside. "This is the Great Hall."

"Wow."

It was an impressive, if not oppressive, room. An enormous gold chandelier hung down from between the large dark beams and decorative white plasterwork panels of the coffered ceiling and hovered over the intricate wooden parquet floor. Vases and painfully tasteful flower arrangements covered polished tables. Louis XIV chairs sat like thrones on either side of a ridiculously over-sized flower arrangement. Gilded clocks perched on enormous mantles. Porcelain and silver posed in small alcoves of deep mahogany. Every inch of it served to remind the visitor of the owner's wealth and power.

"It's beautiful. You know, if you like that sort of thing," Elizabeth said as she sat down in one of the chairs.

"That is William the IV's Coronation chair," Simon said.

Elizabeth sprang out of it with an eep.

Simon laughed and it echoed through the Great Hall. "Don't let it intimidate you. A chair is just a chair."

"If you say so." She nodded toward a row of portraits on the far wall. "Are you in here anywhere?"

"No. Not here. There is one very unfortunate Gainsborough-esque portrait of me as a child complete with blue silks and stockings around here somewhere unless they've burned it."

"They wouldn't do that."

"If there's a God—" Simon started, but was interrupted by the sound of voices and footsteps from above.

"I am not in the habit of repeating myself," Aunt Victoria said as she appeared through the doorway of the minstrels' gallery at the far end of the Great Hall. With that one sentence, all of the air left the room.

"Yes, ma'am." The workman who trailed along behind her bobbed his head with vigorous agreement.

Simon looked up at the gallery. She hadn't changed at all. A bit older, a bit greyer and, if possible, a little harder.

"There is a crack, just there, in the plaster. If you cannot see it please provide me with someone whose vision hasn't been compromised with drink or incompetence."

"Yes, ma'am."

"Good."

"Fasten your seatbelt," Simon said quietly before calling out to the woman on the minstrels' gallery. "Aunt Victoria."

"Oh," Aunt Victoria said, somehow managing to infuse disappointment, disinterest and distaste into the single syllable. She looked down at Simon before her glance flicked to Elizabeth. "You're here."

Simon gritted his teeth. Even though he was the master here, she always made him feel like a small and unwanted child. "It's good to see you too, Aunt Victoria."

"You should have had one of the servants let me know that you'd arrived," she said. "Quite rude."

With one last glare down at them, Aunt Victoria spun around and left the balcony.

"That was chilly," Elizabeth muttered under her breath.

"I think she has ice for blood." His Aunt appeared in the doorway to the great hall and Simon plastered a tight smile onto his face.

Aunt Victoria tilted her head back and narrowed her eyes as she gave Elizabeth an appraising look. Apparently, she didn't like what she found and sniffed in disapproval before turning away and ignoring her completely. Simon felt his blood pressure rise.

"Simon. It's been too long," she said with forced politeness.

"Has it?" Simon said. "Aunt Victoria, this is Elizabeth West. Elizabeth, this is my aunt."

Aunt Victoria's expression soured.

Elizabeth ignored it and smiled politely. "Nice to meet you."

"Yes," Aunt Victoria said. "I'm sure it is." She turned her attention back to Simon. "How long will you be staying?"

"We haven't decided yet." He had intended to spend at least one night here, but now he wasn't sure that was wise. Elizabeth was too good for this place.

Aunt Victoria made a small sound signaling her disapproval. She preferred everything to be planned, predictable, and controllable, preferably by her. It was one of the reasons she so disliked his grandfather Sebastian, her uncle, and one of the very reasons Simon loved him so.

"As you wish," Aunt Victoria said, conceding the battle, but not the war. "Tea is served in the drawing room at four. Please try not to be late."

Simon had a riposte ready, but felt Elizabeth's hand squeeze his.

Aunt Victoria took his silence as assent and glowed in victory. She smiled tightly at Elizabeth. "Welcome to Grey Hall."

After their frosty reception, Simon gave Elizabeth a tour of the estate. She peppered him with questions about every garden and outbuilding. He played the knowledgeable tour guide, but he knew she could tell he was counting the hours until they could leave. After he'd shown her the portrait gallery, including the abomination of him as child where Elizabeth had tried to keep a straight face and failed miserably, he led her to a small, rather unimpressive parlor no one ever used. It was his favorite room in the house.

"I used to come here as a boy."

"It's nice," she said, clearly not seeing the attraction.

Simon held up a finger and grinned. He hadn't shared this secret with anyone. Ever. "Not everything is as it seems. This is my favorite spot in the whole of Grey Hall. "

Lifting up the seat in the bay window, he folded it back like the lid of a trunk. He reached under the edge of the seat and undid a hidden bolt. He pulled the bottom of the cabinet up to reveal a spiral staircase chiseled out of the stone.

Elizabeth's face lit up with delight. "Oh, a secret passage!"

"It's a priest hole," he said as he swung open the front panel to make it easier to enter. "In the 16th century, Queen Elizabeth persecuted Catholics, including passing laws with severe punishments for anyone practicing the faith."

"Recusants."

"Exactly. Many refused to give up their faith and worshipped in secret. Priest holes were hiding places for traveling priests or even used as small chapels. Ours is a bit of both."

Elizabeth leaned forward and tried to see into the darkness.

"It's a wonderful place for hiding things. Very secret," Simon told her.

"Did you hide things down there when you were little?"

"Just myself."

Her face fell and he could tell she was probably imagining him suffering through some sort of horribly Dickensian childhood. Growing up in Grey Hall had been far from ideal, but it was hardly the life of Oliver Twist either. "Every boy needs his own secret kingdom to rule over."

"Can we go in?" she asked.

"It's a bit dusty and cramped."

"I live for dusty and cramped," she said as she started down the stairs.

"Careful," he said grabbing on to her arm. "Let me get a light."

He rummaged around in a drawer and pulled out a flashlight. He checked the batteries. The light was faint. He thumped it on his palm and the light brightened.

"Better let me go first," he said. "Stay close."

The passageway down was narrow and rough. His flashlight danced along the rough-hewn walls as they descended down into the cold, darkness. A very small chamber had been carved at the foot of the stairs. Simon shined his light down a low, arched tunnel that had been chiseled by hand.

Simon felt oddly at home in the bleak little cavern. The boy he had been still lived inside the man.

"Amazing," Elizabeth whispered, gently touching the stone walls. "Imagine how much work went into this, how much they risked to do it."

Most people would have been frightened in a dark, enclosed space like this, but not Elizabeth. She saw it with the same wonder, the same fascination she saw the rest of life.

Simon shined his light toward the far end of the tunnel.

"What's down there?" she asked.

"Dead end." He tried to keep the melancholia from his voice, but failed miserably. Being in Grey Hall again brought back feelings he thought he'd long buried in the past—his guilt over leaving and turning his back on history and heritage, and his anger at himself for feeling guilty at all. He'd run away from this life, but he'd never really been free of it.

Elizabeth stepped closer and wrapped her arms around his waist. "Maybe we can sneak down with spoons and keep digging."

Simon laughed and the sound of it echoed in the small chamber.

"I wonder what these walls have heard?"

"I don't think they're giving up their secrets."

Elizabeth tilted the flashlight up. "Are you?"

Simon shifted uncomfortably. "What do you mean?"

She leaned closer, trying to see his face in the dim light. "You've been acting weird for the last few weeks. What's your secret, Mr. Cross?"

The words he'd been carrying in his heart for the last few weeks almost came out of their own volition, but this wasn't the place. He'd asked her to come to England to show her his past, but more importantly, to ask her to be part of his future. He wanted it to be perfect. She deserved perfect.

His eyes caressed her face and drifted to her cheek. "You've got a little…" He brushed the pad of his thumb against her cheek to wipe away a bit of dirt.

"Better?" Elizabeth said turning her head for inspection.

He nodded and ran his hands down Elizabeth's arms; they were cool to the touch. "You're cold."

He started to rub some warmth into them, but Elizabeth stopped him. She tilted her head up and grew serious. "We don't have to stay here. In Grey Hall I mean. *You* don't have to stay here."

Simon's chest tightened. Of course, she'd understand. "I thought you wanted to see it."

"I did and I have. But when your favorite place in all of glorious Grey Hall is a musty old hole in the ground; that tells me all I need to know about it."

"So many ghosts here," Simon said.

"Maybe it's time to put them to rest?"

"Yes," he said and felt a weight begin to lift. He pulled Elizabeth toward him and held on. Had it been so simple all along? Had all he needed to do was to let go? Or was all he needed was something else to hold on to?

Elizabeth rolled over and felt something poke her cheek. She reached up a still half-asleep hand and rubbed the side of her face. Nothing was there. She opened her eyes and it took her a moment to remember where she was. Little lace curtains fluttered in the breeze through the slightly opened window. She pushed herself up onto her elbow and felt the prickling again. A small feather had escaped from her down pillow. She pulled it out the rest of the way and blew it off her finger. It joined the dust motes as they danced in a shaft of sunlight.

Sebastian's house—Rosewood Cottage.

Yesterday, they'd left Grey Hall and traveled to Hastings. Simon had even spoken with Aunt Victoria before they left. He described it as a very tentative truce, which could mean anything, but it was a step.

Elizabeth stretched and worked out the kinks in her neck. The iron and brass bed gave a protesting creak as she got up. After she dressed, she found the bath just down the hall, splashed cold water on her face and set off to find him.

The house was big, by her standards if not Cross standards, but it felt familiar. She found her way downstairs. A few of the steps of the old wooden staircase squeaked under her feet. Fading, 1930s wallpaper with a small flower motif lined the walls of the hall and an old oriental runner showed the way along the corridor.

"In here," came Simon's voice from down the hall.

Elizabeth found a room with a door slightly ajar and pushed it open the rest of the way. Inside was the absolute, perfect study. The walls were dark wood, but there was plenty of light. An oversized window sat behind a heavy teak desk and tufted leather chair. Brass lamps, bronze statues and rich leather made the room feel warm and solid. The oriental rugs were well worn with tread paths where Sebastian must have paced hour upon hour.

Sitting behind the desk, looking much as she'd imagined Sebastian had at his age, Simon looked up at her from a thick old ledger. "Good morning," he said with a smile. He stood, came around the desk and kissed her. "Sleep well?"

"I did," she said and squinted up at him. "You're in a suspiciously good mood."

"It's this place, I think. It always makes me feel whole again. Even though not every memory here is a good one, this is home."

She knew he was talking about the night his grandfather died. It had been the first secret he'd shared with her, her first glimpse beyond the armor. The pain from his grandfather's death would never be gone, but it didn't define him anymore.

Simon slipped his arms around her waist. "That and the company I keep. And this," he said, stepping away and waving expansively. "This is part of what I've wanted to show you."

It was hard to imagine Simon as a little boy in Grey Hall. It was hard to imagine any little boy in Grey Hall. Sebastian's home was another story entirely. Even though it hadn't been lived in for years, it still echoed with life.

"I used to spend nearly all my time here." Simon pointed to a small secretary's desk and chair off to one side. " That was mine. We'd work here together. He'd give me some sort of task. I doubt I was any real help at all, but he always made me feel part of it. Essential."

Elizabeth had never met Sebastian Cross. Even when they'd both been in 1929 New York, she'd been otherwise occupied as a prisoner on King's yacht. She couldn't imagine how difficult all of it must have been for Simon. She pushed away the memory.

She could see the emotion in his eyes as he nodded and cleared his throat. "Now," he said in control again. "Knowing you, you're in desperate need of coffee."

"That I am."

"The service was supposed to have brought a few basic supplies to the house. Let's see if they did. Kitchen's just down this hall."

After a quick breakfast, Simon showed her around the estate. It was something out of a fairy tale. An arched entrance with a huge old wrought iron gate led into the most charming courtyard she'd ever seen. The gravel road gave way to a circular cobblestone drive lined with box hedges and wild rose bushes. A small group of outbuildings with thatched roofs cozied up to the larger main house and its ivy covered brick walls. Flowerbeds and deep green hedges led to the short path to the front door.

"Beautiful," she said.

"There's quite a bit more to see. And there's something I'd like to show you."

She nodded and he disappeared inside one of the outbuildings. A few moments later she heard a car engine and one of the large barnlike doors flipped open. Simon revved the engine and pulled out into the sunlight. It was the most adorable vintage sports car she'd ever seen—a small silver coupe with large open-mouth grill. An Aston Martin DB5 from the early sixties. Elizabeth whistled in appreciation.

Simon grinned at her from behind the wheel looking more than a little Cary Grantish. "Well, come on."

With a grin to match his, Elizabeth hurried around to the passenger side and slid onto the leather seat, and they drove off down the road. They meandered down winding country lanes, until they crossed an old rutted path with a small cottage at the end. Simon stopped the car.

"That was my great aunt's. She and grandfather were very close. She lived there until she was killed."

"What happened?"

"The Blitz. She joined the Women's Voluntary Service during the war and was killed in a bombing raid in London. He always regretted being overseas at the time and helped fund a small war museum in town in her memory. I think someone comes in to keep the forest from overrunning, but he kept it just as she left it."

They drove for a few more minutes before Simon pulled into a small gravel parking lot near the cliffs above the sea. The early afternoon sun was warm against her skin and she could just barely smell a hint of the ocean on the breeze.

Simon walked her to a group of rocks near the edge of a seaside cliff. Small bits of greenery forced their way out of the rough sandstone and the English Channel stretched beyond the rocky beach below as far as the eye could see. Somewhere in the distance, through the haze, was France, but she couldn't see it.

"Not too close. The rocks give way easily."

Elizabeth didn't have to be told twice. She'd had her fill of rocky cliffs in San Francisco. Simon leaned back against a group of large white rocks.

"I used to come here often as a boy. Most of it's a public park now, but then it was my private playground," he added with a smile. "From here everything seemed possible. I could be anything. Anyone."

"Who did you want to be?"

"A pirate."

The image of little Simon with a striped black and white shirt, red bandana tied over his head and makeshift eye-patch made her smile.

"There used to be quite a few pirates off the coast here."

"Seriously?"

"In the eighteenth century these waters would have been filled with privateers and buccaneers smuggling God knows what."

If she squinted just so, she could just see the tips of tall masts and white sails in the distant whitecaps.

Simon came up behind her and wrapped one arm around her. She leaned back into him.

"Hastings has quite a bit of interesting history. There," Simon said, pointing down the coast, "are the remnants of Hastings Castle built by William of Normandy. And the castle was built on Roman ruins that predate that by another thousand years."

"And I thought the Alamo was old." Elizabeth turned around to face him. "Can we see it? The castle, I mean."

"There's not much left, I'm afraid. Only a few ruins have survived. Several wars, years of neglect and Nazi bombing raids destroyed most of it."

"I'd still like to see it."

Simon nodded. "The past is part of the reason I brought you here. But it's not the only reason."

"You said there was something you wanted to show me."

He pushed himself away from the rocks and fidgeted for a moment. It was strange to see him nervous and unsure. "This," he said. "This is where I come from. This is who I am. Grey Hall, Hastings, all of it. I wanted you to know what's come before so you could decide," he said meeting her eyes, "if you want to be part of what comes next."

Elizabeth's heart stuttered and she felt her pulse race.

"I brought you to this place because, here, I can believe anything's possible. I could even believe a woman like you would want to spend her life with a man like me. Elizabeth—"

CHAPTER THREE

"OY! THIS WAY!" A man wearing plaid tan-and-white shorts and long black socks emerged from the bushes. It was all Elizabeth could do not to strangle him. "Get a move on, we ain't got all day."

The man was soon joined by a plump and panting woman in a loud floral dress and two sullen children who would forever be remembered as the Moment Killers. "You're the one that wanted to see the bloomin' ocean. Get an eyeful 'cause it's the last time I'm taking you sorry lot anywhere."

Elizabeth looked from them back up to Simon willing him to continue. Her head suddenly felt swimmy. He'd been this close, inches away from what she was pretty sure might have been a proposal. She wanted to tell him to ignore them, but the moment was obviously gone. Simon closed his eyes and sighed heavily.

"Simon?" she started, but he shook his head.

"Would you like to see the town?" he asked quietly.

"Pick up your feet!" the mother yelled to her children who were still dawdling behind. She smiled at Simon and Elizabeth. "Beautiful day, innit?"

The father trooped past with a grunt and mumbled, "Mornin'."

Elizabeth smiled through clenched teeth at the invaders. When she turned back, Simon had already started toward the path to the car. All she could do was follow.

The drive into town was quiet. She tried to lose herself in the beautiful scenery, but holy heck, Simon had nearly proposed. She thought briefly about asking him herself. It wasn't as though she hadn't thought about it a thousand times. But Simon was old fashioned and more than that, deep down, she was too. Not that he would have said no if she'd bucked tradition, but she knew that he wanted to be the one, that he needed to be the one, to ask.

The town of Hastings looked and felt wonderfully old, despite a few signs of modern life. Most of the buildings had that wonderful aged patina to their stone facades. The roads were a mixture of brick and cobblestone. If the streets had been empty and a little signage removed, she could have been in Hastings of fifty or even a hundred or more years ago. For the most part, the shops were exactly what you'd find in any tourist center—a mixture of high-priced fashion and home goods and kitschy souvenirs. On their way back toward the town center Simon pointed out a small museum across the street.

"That's what I was telling you about earlier. Grandfather helped fund that as a memorial to Aunt Sybil."

A sweet little old woman greeted them at the door and accepted their donation. The Women in War museum was a small thing, only two rooms, but Elizabeth had always loved local museums. There was a heart and soul that went into them that the larger ones often lacked.

Posters and photographs covered the walls—pictures of women serving tea from mobile canteens or knitting their way to victory. Simon immediately gravitated to a small photograph and plaque that read simply, "In loving memory of Sybil Cross."

Elizabeth had expected Great Aunt Sybil to look like a great aunt, but she didn't. The woman in the photograph couldn't have been much older than Elizabeth. She wore her WVS uniform. Her pin curl hair peeked out from the brim of her cap with the same sort of playfulness she had in her smile. She looked like the sort of woman Elizabeth could have been friends with.

"There's a special hospital exhibit here just for the rest of the week," the woman at the desk said before going back to her book. "You can see it in the back room, if you'd like."

"Thank you," Simon said. He and Elizabeth lingered at Sybil's portrait for a few minutes before moving into the back room.

There were newspaper articles, photographs and even a mannequin wearing a period nurse's uniform. Sections were devoted to the Civil Nursing Reserve, St. Andrew's Ambulance Association and the Women's Voluntary Services. Original reports typed on faded yellow paper told the stories of evacuees brought into the hospitals only to be bombed out again.

Various ringed binders were scattered across the counter with even more photographs. Elizabeth flipped through one. Images of the blitz looked like scenes from a movie. Even though she'd seen massive destruction up close and personal thanks to the 1906 San Francisco earthquake, sometimes it still felt like a dream. Something once removed. The war wasn't fiction though, and every one of the people in the photographs had been real. They'd been standing in those spots just as surely as she was standing in Hastings. She flipped through a few more pages. Newspaper stories of civilian casualties and the difficulties the hospitals endured during the bombing raids. Moving operating theaters to basements and burying radium to keep from contaminating everything with lethal doses of radiation if a bomb should strike. Patients were moved from floor to floor and hospital to hospital trying to stay one step ahead of the Nazi bombs.

In one series of photographs an injured man was being helped into a bed at a new ward at Guy's Hospital in London. The caption read, "Some men lose more than their homes. For some, their identities are stolen by shell shock induced amnesia." The photographer captured a close-up of the man's face. Elizabeth's hands trembled.

"Oh my god," Elizabeth said. "Simon!"

She could barely believe what she was seeing.

Simon came to her side. "What is it?"

She pointed at the man in the photograph. "Look."

The man in the photograph looked confused and in some pain, but there was no mistaking who he was. It was Evan Eldridge.

Chapter Four

"Dear God," Simon said, leaning closer for a better look. "Is that...?"

"Mr. Eldridge."

When Elizabeth had traveled back to 1906, she'd stayed at the Eldridges' home. She'd spent weeks there and hour after hour in the parlor where Evan Eldridge's portrait hung. She'd heard the pain in Mrs. Eldridge's voice as she recounted the last time she'd seen her husband. She'd said it was her worst nightmare come true. He'd been a member of the Council for Temporal Studies for years and been on countless missions through time, just like Simon's grandfather. Until one day, he left and never returned. Mrs. Eldridge had always assumed he'd been killed, but the man in the photograph was quite alive. At least, he was alive in the 1940s.

"When is this?" Elizabeth asked as she scanned the text next to the photograph. "I don't see any dates."

She picked up the binder and took it into the front room. "I'm sorry to bother you," she said as she placed it in front of the woman at the desk. "Do you know anything about these? These photographs? When they were taken?"

The woman put on her glasses. "Hmmm. No, just what it says there. Something about Guy's Hospital. It was a feature in the Times, I think." She flipped through a few more pages and pointed to a small news clipping. "Yes, there we are. September 18, 1942, Guy's Hospital. Poor man appears to be suffering from a case of amnesia. It wasn't uncommon. All that bombing, it's a miracle anyone kept their wits about them."

"Yes," Elizabeth said, her heart racing almost as quickly as her thoughts. "Thank you. I don't suppose we can have a copy of this?"

"I'm afraid we don't have the facilities for that."

Maybe it was available online? Most of the newspapers had digital archives now. Of course, she didn't have her computer and she knew Sebastian's home didn't have wireless anyway. Surely, there was a cyber-café in town.

She grabbed Simon's hand and dragged him out onto the sidewalk. "Where's the closest Internet café?"

"Tell me you're not seriously considering traveling back in time, " he said in a strained, hushed voice, "into a war zone, for God's sake, to virtually kidnap a man we've never even met."

"I am."

The vein in Simon's temple started to visibly throb. "Let's discuss this at home," he said with great effort. "Please? We agreed it was better to not know what happened to the people we left in the past."

At the time, she'd agreed, but her initial resolve had lasted a whole two weeks, which was actually a week longer than she thought it would last. She'd looked up Charlie Blue from their trip to 1929 New York, but she never did find anything. She'd managed not to look up Teddy or Max. Yet.

"This is different," she said.

Simon narrowed his eyes.

"It is. First of all, we didn't leave him in the past. He was part of the future when we were in the past and now that we're in the future, he's part of our past, but it isn't the same past, so it doesn't count."

"Elizabeth."

"Don't 'Elizabeth' me right now. You can't tell me what we just saw doesn't bother you."

Simon looked around anxiously and took her by the arm. "Of course it does," he said. "But there's nothing we can do to change it now."

"That's just it. We can."

Simon stopped walking. "We shouldn't."

"Why? He doesn't belong there and you know it."

"I don't know anything of the sort and neither do you. We have to believe this is how things are meant to be. Anything else is madness, Elizabeth."

"Then color me mad." That garnered her a few glances from passersby.

Simon waited until they were alone again. "Elizabeth."

"We have the watch. We know where and when he is. How can we *not* do something to help?"

The drive back to the cottage was a silent one. All Elizabeth could think about was the last time they'd had a conversation like this. The Council had asked for her help and she'd blindly trusted them. She and Simon fought; she left; he followed. He should have listened to her and, as it turned out, she should have listened to him. The last thing she wanted was a repeat performance. If they were going to do this thing, they had to do it together or not at all.

Simon opened one of the bottles of wine they'd picked up at the market. It was starting to get chilly outside as the sun set, and he built a small fire in the grate in the parlor. Elizabeth slipped off her shoes and tucked her legs under her on the plush sofa. Simon sat opposite her in a large overstuffed chair. The silence sat everywhere else.

Elizabeth took a sip of wine and looked into the glass for inspiration. She had an army of arguments ready to march, but she was afraid none of them would make any difference. Simon wasn't exactly a fan of time travel. He'd made that clear enough. Several times. How could she possibly convince him it was the right thing to do? Despite the danger. Despite the insanity of it all.

She took another sip and wondered if you could get Dutch courage from French wine. "Simon," she started. "I know it's crazy."

"Completely. Certifiably." He noticed her frown and lifted his hands in apology. "I'm listening," he said.

"All right. First of all, we know the Council isn't going to help, even though they should. They've proven that "no man left behind" isn't exactly their company motto. And that leaves us. We are, literally, the only people who can."

"Yes, just because you can doesn't mean you should."

"I'll get to the should in a minute. Just wait. Second of all, it's not like last time or the time before. We know exactly what we need to do and where and when to do it. Thirdly, there's no King Kashian or Madame Petrovka. There's no big bad."

"Excepting the Nazis, of course."

Elizabeth paused. "Okay, I'll give you that one. But, we'll be in London, well after the Blitz, so it's not like we'll be jumping right into the middle of the Battle of the Bulge or something."

"The Battle of Britain, no, of course not, just right into the middle of a city ravaged by years of war and still bombed on a regular basis."

"A little research and we'll know what's safe and what isn't. And, we'd only have to stay long enough to get Evan out of the hospital. We can plan it so that we're in and out in just a few days."

Simon thought about it for a moment. "You're assuming there's an eclipse shortly after our arrival that we can use for our return."

"Well, yeah."

Obviously he remained unconvinced, but he had promised to hear her out and was true to his word. "All right. And the should?"

Elizabeth sat forward. "You feel it too, Simon. I know you do. It's the right thing to do. It's dangerous. It might even be crazy. I'll admit that. But that doesn't change the fact that there's a man who needs our help and a woman who deserves it."

Time for the trump card. "If positions were reversed," she said. "If Evan saw a picture of you or me trapped in the past, injured and lost, what would you want him to do? Would you want him to say it wasn't his business? That it wasn't worth the risk?"

Simon stared at her for a long moment and then set down his wine glass. Finally, he stood and walked over to the window. "I think you know the answer to that."

She joined him at the window. "Then is it right to expect to receive what we aren't willing to give?"

She put her hand on his arm and urged him to turn around and face her. "We'll be all right."

"You sound awfully certain."

"I am. It's one of the pleasant byproducts of being delusional."

Simon laughed briefly and then grew serious again. "This isn't so simple."

"I know. But it's the right thing to do, and we both know it."

CHAPTER FIVE

THE NEXT SEVERAL DAYS were a flurry of research, argument and planning. Simon hadn't been pleased that she'd brought the watch with them to England. When she'd explained that it wasn't something to be left lying around, especially not with a Council that Should Not Be Trusted lurking about, he'd agreed, reluctantly.

When it came to the research, Simon was deep in his element. He'd learned quite a bit from his last experience preparing for a trip back in time. He prepared a list of items they'd need including: passports, identity cards, and ration books.

Despite how exacting the records from the period were, there were still blind spots - little things like bombing raids. It certainly wouldn't be anywhere near as dangerous as London during the Blitz when the Nazis bombed England for nine months straight and the city itself for 57 consecutive nights. 1942 wouldn't be half as bad as the later period of the war, when the Nazis resumed bombings with doodlebugs and V-2s. It was a relative lull, but there was no way they could tell when and where each and every bombing raid took place. In the end, they had to be satisfied with a good idea of what sections survived unscathed. If they stuck to them, they should be all right.

Clothing and other supplies were fairly easy to come by. Even forging documents of the period was simple enough. National identity cards were readily available on eBay and collectors and replica makers had every bit of ephemera they could possibly need including passports, travel papers and War Department Identity Cards. Manipulating them to add their real names and photographs was simple enough.

They'd just returned from a shopping excursion when Elizabeth noticed a large vase overflowing with yellow and white roses on their front doorstep. She carried it inside as Simon took their packages into the study.

"Should I be jealous?" Simon said.

"The question is, should I?" Elizabeth handed him the attached notecard. "It's addressed to you."

Simon sat down behind the desk. Elizabeth put the vase on a side table.

"They're from Aunt Victoria," he said. "A peace offering."

Elizabeth rearranged a few of the flowers and pricked her finger on one. "With thorns. Now, that's what I call passive-aggressive."

Simon laughed. "Are you all right?"

"As long as they haven't been dipped in poison."

Simon got up from the desk. " Let me see."

Elizabeth held out her finger. Simon examined it with excessive care and rubbed her hand gently before kissing her palm. "Does it hurt?" He kissed the inside of her wrist.

Her cheeks flushed. He knew what kissing her there did to her. "No," she said. "But it hurts a little here." She pointed to her bottom lip.

Simon leaned forward, his eyes dipped down to her mouth and back up. "Here?" he said before he took her mouth in a gentle, tugging kiss.

Elizabeth let out a shuddering breath. "And other places."

He kissed her neck. "I'm afraid this requires," he said punctuating each phrase with another kiss, "further investigation."

"Thorough," Elizabeth said between gasping breaths. "Thorough investigation."

Simon's hands pulled her body against his and the phone rang. He pulled back and was about to go in for another kiss when the phone rang again. "Bugger."

He let her go and went to the desk. "Remember where I was."

Elizabeth wasn't about to forget, but the call wasn't a quick one and the moment was gone. The man on the phone was one of the currency collectors they'd contacted. Simon insisted that they buy an obscene amount of currency. He'd traveled as a pauper once and had no intention of repeating the experience. In any period, money was their most useful tool.

Simon had tried to explain early English currency. In 1971, the UK and Ireland had adopted decimalization, so that everything was based on units of ten and one hundred. That made sense. Pre-Decimalization money, the sort they'd be using, did not. Twelve pence in a shilling and twenty shillings in a pound, half-pennies, farthings, half-crowns and tanners and dozens of other coins and bills had left her completely and utterly lost.

She'd have an easier time keeping their cover story straight than their money. They decided to keep the backstory simple. She and Simon were newlyweds, now living in America. They'd seen the photograph of Evan, Elizabeth's uncle, in the paper and had come to collect him.

The real trick for their cover story had been finding a compelling reason Simon wasn't serving his country in the war. By 1942, every able-bodied man in England under the age of 51 would have been in the service. Special exemptions were given to a few categories of men, including those in the employ of a foreign government. That meant Simon was a professor working with the American government on some top-secret projects for the Department of

Substitute Materials, whatever that was. The simpler the story the better. Luckily, without computers and long distance calls being rather expensive, it was doubtful anyone would or even could do much checking up on them. They were also counting on the fact that the hospital beds were at a premium and the administrators would be inclined to release Evan without much ado just to free one up.

A penumbral eclipse that would allow the watch to activate was just three days away. Simon and Elizabeth planned to arrive in London on September 18, 1942, the day the photograph of Evan was taken. A return eclipse was less than a week later. It all sounded doable. Even though she knew it was dangerous, Elizabeth couldn't hide her excitement. Given the chance, who wouldn't want to travel in time? See history as it really was? In spite of the dangers they'd faced and the ones she was sure would surprise them this time, she counted herself incredibly privileged to be able to go. Even though he blustered on about the risks, she knew Simon felt the same way. Deep, deep Marianas Trench down.

The night before the eclipse Elizabeth woke from a strange dream. Memories of it disappeared like smoke as she got her bearings. She rolled over to snuggle up to Simon, but his side of the bed was empty and cold. She slipped on her robe and headed down to the study. The light from inside stretched out into the hallway.

Simon sat reading in Sebastian's overstuffed club chair and he lifted his eyes from the pages when she padded in. It wasn't unusual for him to get up in the middle of the night and go into his study at home and read until the early morning hours.

"What are you reading?"

He held up the book for her to see. "Churchill."

Elizabeth read the spine. "The Gathering Storm. That sounds ominous."

"It was. It is." He closed the book and set it aside. "Are you sure about this?"

Elizabeth thought about it. She owed him and herself that. "Yes. Are you having doubts?"

Simon let out a sigh. "Plagues of them," he said as he stood. "And yet, I think we're doing the right thing. As insane as it is."

"Those are the best kind of things." She took his hand. "Come back to bed. Churchill can wait."

They went to bed and managed a few hours of sleep before the day came. Simon finished his preparations, leaving Elizabeth in charge of packing. The smart time traveler travels light, but smashing everything two people would need for an entire week into one leather valise was easier said than done. Somehow, she managed it though. Her pocketbook, a simple shoulder bag, was crammed with money, coin purse, papers, handkerchief, small pad and pencil stub, lipstick, compact and a vintage Victorinox Swiss Army Knife.

Elizabeth had never been one to wear much jewelry, but she did slip on a long silver necklace with a small key as the pendant. It had been a gift from Teddy, the watchmaker, and it just felt right to wear it when they traveled. Other than that, the only bit of jewelry needed was the wedding ring she was supposed to wear as part of their cover, which Simon had promised to take care of, but still hadn't produced.

The suitcase packed, Elizabeth looked at herself in the mirror. A woman from the 1940's looked back. Her hair came down just below her shoulders in large lazy waves. The clothing was simple. She wore a blue cotton floral print dress, sensible, clunky brown Mary Janes and a tweed overcoat. She'd meant to ask Simon to draw the seam of her nonexistent stockings down the back of her legs, but in the rush of the coming eclipse, she'd forgotten.

She grabbed the suitcase and went to look for Simon. She found him in the living room going over their papers one last time. He looked every inch the part in his wool trousers, oxford cloth shirt, brown sweater vest, jacket and fedora.

"You should wear more hats," she said.

Simon turned to her and smiled as he tugged on the brim. "I actually quite like it. Are you ready? If you have any doubts—"

"I don't." She took his hand in hers. "It'll be all right."

"One last thing." Simon reached into his jacket pocket and pulled out two simple gold rings.

"Those look familiar," she said. They looked remarkably like the bands they'd used in New York when they'd first traveled back in time, when they'd first fallen in love. Of course, those had been fake gold and these were definitely not fake.

"Yes," Simon said nervously. "Don't they?"

He slipped the ring onto her finger and her heart skipped a beat. Even knowing it wasn't real, they weren't really married, just the image of him putting the ring on her finger made her feel flushed. Simon quickly put on his own before busying himself with the watch and making sure the coordinates were properly set for the arrival. "It's nearly time."

Elizabeth stared at the ring and felt a smile tug at her lips. It wasn't just similar to the one from New York. It *was* the same ring. The big old softy. "Simon?"

He held the watch in one hand and took hold of hers with the other. He studied the ring on her finger for a moment before looking at her with such a mixture of regret and longing it made her heart ache.

Before either of them could say what was on their minds, the blue light came. It snaked up his arm and down hers and they were both frozen as time and the world shattered around them.

It was dark, in the forest at night dark. They'd planned on arriving at night in a secluded section of St. James Park near Buckingham Palace. It was one of the few places in London that offered some cover and, at night, it wasn't likely to be too busy.

"Are you all right?" Simon asked as he held her elbow to steady her.

It took Elizabeth a few seconds to unscramble her brains. "You?"

"Yes," Simon said as he looked around to make sure their arrival had gone unseen.

They weren't alone in the park, but they'd landed in the middle of a copse of plane trees obscuring them from view. Luckily, it was so dark that unless they'd landed smack on top of someone it was doubtful they would have been seen anyway.

Simon studied her face, assuring himself she was steady enough and stepped away from the cover of the trees. He walked out onto the path and Elizabeth followed.

He took a few steps in one direction before stopping. "Strange sensation. It's the same, and yet, it isn't." He turned around to get his bearings and must have seen something he recognized. "It's this way, I think," Simon said pointing toward a path that disappeared deeper into the park.

The "it" was the Ritz. One of Simon's conditions was that if they were going to do this, they were going to do it in style. She'd survived her trip to Grey Hall, so she was pretty sure she could deal with the Ritz. It was a strange awakening, realizing that there were levels of posh she'd thought existed only in books and fairy tales. But then, before Simon, she'd thought the Best Western in Amarillo was the height of luxury. Maybe her frame of reference was a bit askew.

As though Simon could hear her thoughts, he gave her hand a reassuring squeeze. The moon was bright enough to light their path and they made their way down the wide colonnade to the northern edge of the park. After a few minutes, they emerged onto one of London's main thoroughfares, the Mall. Elizabeth had seen it in documentaries and footage of processions from

Buckingham Palace which was just up the road. But it certainly didn't look like this.

Even though it wasn't really all that late, just after nine o'clock if all went as planned, it was difficult to see. She'd read about the blackout, but nothing prepared her for the reality of it. Even before the war, the Air Ministry issued strict regulations regarding lights at night. Every window was covered; every streetlamp and outside light was kept off. The goal was total darkness so that enemy planes couldn't use ground landmarks to navigate to their targets. In the world before GPS, if all the pilots saw below was a featureless darkness, they'd have virtually no way of knowing if they were over their intended target or not.

The blackout was serious business and heavy fines were levied for letting even the smallest chink of light escape into the night. The result was a city plunged into total and complete darkness, save for the moon when it broke through the clouds. There was absolutely no ambient light, not from windows or streetlamps or even cigarettes. Or cars.

She heard the car before she saw it. It was as black as the night around it and it was nearly on top of her before she realized how close she'd come to it.

"Be careful," Simon said. "They can barely see us." As if to illustrate his point, two more large army trucks sped past like hulking metal shadows.

The streets were bustling with people, but there was an odd hushed quality to it, like everyone was holding their breath. It reminded Elizabeth of the blackout she'd experienced after an earthquake in Southern California a few years back. London had that same dreamlike feeling to it.

Elizabeth stood on the sidewalk and had to pause a moment to take it all in. Her eyes had finally adjusted to the darkness. The skies were fairly clear and in the distance she could see several large, silver blimp-like things hanging in the air with long tethers keeping them in place.

"Barrage balloons," Simon explained following her gaze. "They keep the bombers from flying low. The higher they have to fly, the more difficult it is to target effectively. It might look a bit odd, but they are pretty damn useful."

She listened for the drone of a fighter plane and watched for the shaft of light from a searchlight on the ground, but none came. At least, not yet.

As they walked up the Mall and turned off onto the side streets toward Mayfair and the hotel, they saw more and more people. The few pedestrians became a stream and the random car became many. Bicyclists darted in and out of traffic in the darkness. One narrowly escaped being clipped by a passing car. Forget the bombs, the blackout itself was dangerous.

The blackout gave everything a surreal quality. Add to that, tall piles of sandbags that created makeshift bunkers around a huge anti-aircraft gun emplacement and Elizabeth felt a chill that had nothing to do with the night air.

An older man in a dark blue uniform and wide-brimmed helmet with a large "W" stenciled on it walked down the street, inspecting each building he passed. "Best get inside," he said to them. "I have the feeling Jerry's restless tonight."

"Warden," Simon said with a nod.

Just as it was before, that first contact with someone from the actual time period grounded her in the new reality. Before that, Elizabeth felt like she was walking around a set where everything was just a façade. It was the people that made it all real. How those people adapted to hardship and how bizarre and frightening things became everyday occurrences had always fascinated Elizabeth. Now, she was going to get a chance to see it play out firsthand. Except for the dark and the giant gun, everything seemed almost normal.

The buildings they passed were mostly large four and five story buildings, lots of them hotels, with impressive gray stone fronts and elaborate black wrought iron railings and embellishments. They had a timeless elegance about them, except for the one with an enormous bomb crater carving out the bottom two stories.

They traveled a few more blocks before making a left.

"Piccadilly," Simon said.

"Why aren't there any street signs?" She'd noticed early on that nothing was marked. Whenever she went to a new town, she always did her best to get the lay of the land, but here it wasn't going to be easy.

"They were all removed at the start of the war, in case of invasion. Why make it easy for the enemy to find where they want to go? Anyone who's supposed to be here knows where everything is."

"Except me," she said, pulling her coat more tightly around her.

"That's why you've got me," Simon said with a smile and then looked ahead and nodded. "Ah, there it is."

He gestured toward a block-sized building that appeared to have been transported directly from Paris. A huge arcade served as a covered walkway and ran the length of the building. In the darkness, she could just make out an unlit set of Broadway-like lights above the first arch that spelled out "THE RITZ."

Sticky tape crisscrossed the glass windows and doors and blackout blinds kept any light inside. The doorman was an older gentleman, his suit a little threadbare. Elizabeth noticed a helmet and rucksack next to the door. Probably working double duty in the home guard. Elizabeth had read that all fit men between the ages of 18 and 51 were serving their country. That left boys and old men to do everything else.

She smiled at the doorman as he opened the main door to the lobby for them and they stepped inside a dark vestibule with large black drapes keeping the bright lights from the lobby away from the open door.

Moving from the dark entryway into the lobby was like Dorothy landing in Oz. The muted grays and blacks outside were replaced by vivid colors—blazingly bright candelabra sconces, enormous vaulted marble walls and an ornate gold and red carpet were a shock to the system. Cigarette smoke drifted up through the open domed ceiling and into the grand staircase spiraling several stories above.

The room was packed. The lobby was a knot of uniforms, expensive suits and stylish dresses. No hoi polloi here.

Simon led Elizabeth to a relatively quiet corner and put down their suitcase. She was glad for the break. They hadn't walked very far, and yet, her sensible shoes were doing unpleasant things to her feet. She managed to slide out of one just a touch and wiggle her foot to get the blood flowing again.

"Wait here," Simon said. "I'll see what I can do about a room."

Elizabeth looked at the crush of people near the front desk. It didn't look promising. "Good luck," she said and watched him navigate his way through the crowd.

"He's gonna need it," a voice said behind her with what was clearly not a British accent. It sounded mid-western.

Elizabeth turned around and saw, leaning against one of the marble columns, a man in a dark gray suit lighting a cigarette. He slipped the lighter into his jacket pocket and pulled out a pack of Lucky Strike and offered her one.

"No, thank you," Elizabeth said.

The man took a deep drag of his cigarette, put the pack away and blew the smoke toward the ceiling. He was nice looking and the sort who knew it too, but not in an "I'm too sexy for your air-raid" sort of way, just a casual confidence. He had a square jaw, short black hair and a dark complexion. He was, literally, tall, dark and handsome. "You're American. It's nice to see a fellow Yank."

She'd only been gone from America for a few days, but hearing his accent was strangely comforting. Little familiar things must have meant so much to the soldiers who were away from home for years at a time. Elizabeth smiled and tried to get her rogue shoe back on.

He held out his hand. "Name's Jack Wells. Chicago."

He seemed genuine enough and he had a nice smile. Her two litmus tests for people were their handshakes and their smiles. He passed on both counts. "Elizabeth We—…Cross. Elizabeth Cross. Texas." She was really going to have to get used to saying it.

"Newlywed?" he asked, as he leaned back against the pillar. "Hell of a place for a honeymoon."

"Simon and I, well, it's sort of family business." The shoe was getting away from her now. She tried to look casual as she reached out with her toe to drag it back. "We're only here for a little while."

"Aren't we all?" he said, his smile fading just around the edges.

The sincerity and hint of pain in his voice made her forget the shoe for an instant and that was all it took. A large group of men passed by and the one in the lead stepped on her sensible shoe and took a header right onto the plush oriental carpet. What happened next was a blur. The man on the ground rolled over and pulled a long-nosed pistol from beneath the huge pile of medals on his chest and pointed it right at her. Before she had a chance to react three of the other men had stepped between them and leveled ugly and enormous sawed-off shotguns right at her head.

CHAPTER SIX

LIZABETH'S ARMS SHOT UP over her head in the most immediate
surrender ever. "I'm sorry!"

The men with the guns were shouting at her in some language
she didn't recognize. The one she'd tripped had been helped up
and was in turn yelling at them and waving his pistol around like
he was going to shoot out every light in the room. People near
them chattered in excitement. Next to her, Jack had his arms raised
too, but he looked incredibly unconcerned and maybe even a little
amused.

The one she'd tripped looked like something out of a Mel
Brooks movie, which would have been hilarious if her heart weren't
lodged in her throat. Her life, which was more of a short than a
feature, flashed before her eyes. The man jabbed his gun toward her
and berated one of the men at his side. The large golden starburst
medals on his chest dangled from ribbons almost as bilious as his
uniform. Epaulets the size of dinner plates with long fringe shook
as he straightened his back, re-holstered his gun and regained his
composure with a haughty flourish.

"It's all right!" Jack yelled above the din. When the bodyguards shifted their attention to him, he added, "*Il s'agissait d'un accident. Sa chaussure. Erreur.* False alarm. It's all right!"

That seemed to instantly deflate the interest of the crowd, but the effect wasn't so immediate on the men with the big guns. Elizabeth kept her eyes trained on the men and their guns, mostly the guns.

"Elizabeth!" That was Simon's voice. He was somewhere in the crowd, but she didn't dare look away.

Two of the men with shotguns stepped forward and crowded Elizabeth into the wall. One of them grabbed her arm. "You will come with us."

Jack quickly stepped between them and eased the man's hand off her arm. "It was an accident. We're very sorry, your majesty. *Il s'agissait d'un accident.* Please accept our apologies. *Unë jam i keq.*"

Elizabeth's stomach did a half-gainer. Your majesty? Of course. She'd managed to trip a king.

The bodyguards glared at them both. His majesty said something to them in a language Elizabeth didn't recognize—it sounded like a mixture of Russian, Greek and somewhere in the Middle East—and the two men stepped back making room for the king.

Jack bowed deeply at the waist. "Your Majesty," he said and gave Elizabeth a good sharp jab in the ribs. "Your Majesty."

She curtseyed quickly and kept her eyes deferentially glued to the floor. "I'm sorry, Your Majesty. I'm really, really sorry." She'd been in London for less than an hour and she'd already insulted a king and had guns pulled on her. Simon was never going to let her forget this one.

Jack said something in French to the men. They frowned in unison. He pointed toward her shoe that had skittered across the floor and come to rest at the edge of the gathered crowd.

Simon finally pushed his way through the crowd just as Jack pointed to her shoe. He knelt down and picked it up. Cautiously he brought it back to Elizabeth. "What have you done?" he said under his breath.

Jack continued to explain in French and eventually the king narrowed his eyes and then huffed out an indignant breath. Jack spoke very quickly. One year of high school French wasn't helping Elizabeth very much, but apparently, Simon could understand and something Jack said made him swallow a laugh.

The king arched his back and tugged at the end of his perfectly waxed mustache, but listened with growing interest. He wasn't exactly warming up, but whatever Jack said brought out the gentleman in him and some sort of agreement was reached. The king regarded her briefly. His foppish outfit and ridiculous frown faded away and she saw the sincere man beneath. The human connection flickered and died and the supreme ruler returned. He gave her a perfunctory bow, waved his hand at his entourage and then continued on his way as though nothing had happened.

Jack waited until the king and his retinue were out of earshot before turning to Elizabeth and Simon. He stuck out his hand. "You must be Simon. I'm Jack."

Simon warily shook his hand. "Would someone like to tell me what in God's name just happened?" He turned to Elizabeth and held out the offending shoe.

Elizabeth took it sheepishly. "It slipped." She held onto Simon's shoulder for balance while she slipped her shoe back on. "Who was that I almost killed and who almost killed me?"

"The King of Albania," Jack said. "He's wound a little tight, but after a few dozen assassination attempts, I would be too."

Elizabeth went cold. She was lucky he hadn't shot her, or had her shot, or imprisoned in some Albanian castle. Did Albania have castles? Where was Albania anyway?

"Are you all right?" Simon asked.

"I'm okay, just the first time I've tripped a king." She exhaled at the thought.

Jack laughed. "You made quite an impression."

"She always does," Simon said. "Thank you for interceding on her behalf. But about that last bit…"

Jack tugged on his ear. "Yeah, I might have gotten carried away there. But, it was that or the firing squad."

Elizabeth couldn't tell if he was joking or not. Her heart had only just finished its drum solo. "What last bit?"

"My French is a little rusty," Simon said, "but I think he said that you were pregnant and as a grateful gesture for his beneficence would name the child after him."

"I'm afraid to ask," Elizabeth said.

Jack winced. "Zog."

"Come again?"

Jack laughed. "That's his name. King Zog."

"Well, it is memorable." In a "please push me off the jungle gym" sort of way.

"In a matter of mere minutes," Simon said, "you managed to cause an international incident and relegate our poor future child to a life of hardship and ridicule. That's impressive by any standards."

"It's these darn sensible shoes!" she said wiggling the offensive footwear.

"Well, you'd better find a way to keep them on your feet, I'm afraid. Even before your exchange with the king, we were sadly out of luck here. No rooms. We might try Claridge's."

Jack shook his head. "The city's lousy with royals in exile, generals, diplomats and Romanovs who may or may not be Romanovs. Be the same story at Claridge's. You can try, but forget the Savoy, Grosvenor House, Berkeley and the Dorchester too."

"There must be something," Elizabeth said. That was one of the problems with time travel; it was impossible to make reservations.

"You might try Browns or Dukes. They might have something, but really you're better off in Knightsbridge or Kensington. Won't be as posh, but it's not too bad."

"What do you think?" Elizabeth asked Simon.

"I'm not sure we have much choice in the matter. I should have realized the hotels would be like this."

"We did have a lot on our minds."

Jack cleared his throat uncomfortably. He must have thought she was referring to their wedding night. The realization made Elizabeth blush, which only made matters worse.

"There's my date," Jack said with a grin. He smiled down at Elizabeth. "It was fun."

From the gleam in his eye, he really meant that. "Thank you," she said and then placed her hand over her stomach. "And little Zog thanks you too."

Jack laughed and shook hands again with Simon. He picked up his overcoat from the back of a chair and waved toward a leggy redhead across the room. His date was apparently Jessica Rabbit. He took a few steps away and turned back and said, "Keep your head down and your shoes on, all right?"

Elizabeth watched Jack disappear into the crowd and turned to Simon.

"Ready?" Simon said as he picked up their suitcase. He gestured for her to go first and followed her toward the door. "Fictional or not. We are not naming our baby Zog."

By the time they'd walked to Knightsbridge, Elizabeth's feet genuinely hurt, but there was no way she was taking her shoes off in public, no matter how much they ached. They passed by

Harrod's Department Store and Simon promised they'd try to get her a new pair in the morning.

The first two bedsits were full and it was well after ten in the evening when they finally found a small room to rent at a bed and breakfast. The carpet was loud and the walls were quiet, but it was clean and available. The furnishings were simple, but functional. One hard occasional chair that had seen more than the occasional visitor huddled next to a small table. A small dressing table and a wardrobe that had definite left leanings took up the rest of the room.

After settling in and cleaning up a bit, it was late and the lumpy double-bed and scratchy starched sheets looked pretty appealing. They shared the bath down the hall with the other five people on their floor, every one of whom seemingly had to go at the same time as she did. Elizabeth waited in line in the hall and made small talk with a woman who'd been bombed out twice already—once during the blitz and again a few weeks ago.

Finally, it was Elizabeth's turn and she washed up quickly in the cold bathroom and even colder water. By this time, the hot water was long gone. She said her goodnights to the rest of the line and hurried down the cold dark hall to their cold dark room.

Simon was just getting into bed when she came in.

"All right?" he asked as he pulled back the covers.

"Cold." Elizabeth took off her overcoat that was subbing for a robe and laid it over the back of the chair.

"What on earth are you wearing?"

Elizabeth did her best imitation of a fifties pin-up. "Do you like it?"

"It's entirely impractical and hardly period," he said with a frown as his eyes took in all she had to offer. "And, yes, very much."

Elizabeth giggled and dove under the covers. The room had a small radiator, but it only gave off heat for a whopping two-foot radius. "The other one was too long. I'd wake up strangled by my own clothes."

Simon started to argue the logic of that statement, but apparently thought better of it. Judging from his expression, he was definitely pleasantly surprised by her clothes or lack of them.

"Besides, the other one barely fit in the suitcase. This one takes up hardly any room at all."

Simon grinned. "In that case." He slid under the covers next to her.

Elizabeth cuddled up to Simon's warmth. He always ran hot and she loved curling up next to him.

"Good Lord!" he said. "Your feet are like bricks of ice."

"I know," Elizabeth said as she rubbed them against the warmth of his legs.

"Stop that."

Elizabeth settled for rubbing her feet against the sheets instead and snuggled up against Simon's side. Her left hand came to rest on his chest and the wedding ring caught the light from the bedside lamp. She rubbed the band with her thumb.

"Feels odd, doesn't it, to be wearing these again?"

Simon didn't reply at first. After a moment, he covered her hand with his. "Does it?"

"Just that these are the same rings and this room is a lot like that first room we shared in New York. It's all the same and yet completely different."

His long fingers traced random patterns on the back of her hand.

Elizabeth rolled over and edged her way onto his chest, resting her head on her laced hands. "I'm glad we're here. I know what we're doing is the right thing. But more than that I'm glad we're here together."

Simon caressed her cheek gently. "I wouldn't have it any other way. I don't want it *to be* any other way."

Elizabeth closed the gap of inches that separated them and kissed him. She would never get tired of the way he held her when they kissed. Strong and loving, passionate and gentle. It was the safest place on earth.

After a moment, Simon leaned over and shut off the light plunging them into complete darkness. The blackout curtains on the windows kept out any ambient light and only the thinnest sliver of light from the hall crept under the door. The darkness was so absolute it made her shiver.

Simon kissed her again. "All right?"

She'd never been scared of the dark before, but then she'd never experienced dark quite like this. Putting aside the idea that she'd discovered a latent phobia, Elizabeth returned Simon's kiss and settled into his arms, but the chill of the dark never quite went away.

CHAPTER SEVEN

ELIZABETH WASN'T A FAN of hospitals, even modern day ones. She'd always envisioned older hospitals as a cross between a torture chamber and a Romanian insane asylum. Guy's Hospital wasn't nearly that bad. The nurses' uniforms were crisp and white and they even wore little pinafore aprons and caps that looked like miniature nun's habits. Guy's was orderly and enormous, but she was still glad she wasn't a patient there. Germs were waging their own war in the hospital wards. Sanitary conditions had a long way to go and antibiotics hadn't even been discovered yet.

Despite all of that, Guy's was impressive. At least a dozen interconnected buildings sat behind a huge expanse of lawn and a forbidding, spiked iron gate. Inside it was cavernous and dark and overflowing with patients. It took them quite a while to find the wing that held patients with head injuries. When they saw men shuffling down the corridors in white gowns with huge bandage turbans on their heads, they knew they'd come to the right place.

It was more than a little horrifying, but Elizabeth managed to concentrate on the mission, on why they'd come. Somewhere in this enormous place was Evan Eldridge and they were there to bring him home. After a few inquiries, they were finally directed to an office in the Southwark Wing and any dreams of walking out the door with Evan today were immediately dashed. Present or past, red tape was red tape, and apparently, the English took great comfort in the structure it provided.

"We're here to see a patient. An older man about six feet, silver hair?" Elizabeth asked the duty nurse.

The woman didn't look up from her paperwork. "Name?"

"He has a head injury, I'm not sure he remembers it," Elizabeth said.

"Name?"

"Evan Eldridge."

The nurse flipped through the pages of a large ledger, made a short notation and then held up a clipboard with a raft of papers. "Fill these out."

"He is here then?" She'd been so afraid that his memory was completely lost. It was wonderful news if he remembered his name.

The nurse nodded and held out the clipboard.

"Thank you."

She and Simon sat in the waiting room and filled out form after form. After returning those to the nurse, they were told the paperwork would have to be reviewed by his doctor and the Consultant, who was apparently the big cheese. If they were lucky, they might get to see Evan tomorrow, but there weren't any guarantees.

Impatient and worried that they wouldn't meet their deadline, the eclipse that would take them home was just a few days away, Simon insisted on seeing the Consultant. Twenty minutes later a small round man with small round glasses agreed to see them.

His office looked like a filing cabinet had exploded. Stacks of folders and papers covered nearly every inch of available floor and desk space. He waved them in and moved stacks of papers that covered the guest chairs.

"Please," he said gesturing toward two old wooden chairs. "You'll have to forgive the state of things. The filing room caught fire and these are the refugees."

"It's quite all right," Simon said as they took their seats. "Thank you for seeing us, Doctor…"

"Newman. I'm not sure I'll be of much help. The administration is rather firm on release policies."

"I understand, but we're under a bit of a timeline. We have return tickets on a clipper to the United States next week and, as you can imagine, they're rather difficult to come by."

"I should imagine." Dr. Newman dug through a pile of folders. "Eldridge, wasn't it?"

"Yes," Elizabeth said. "Evan Eldridge."

The doctor skimmed the file. "Hmm. Head injury, intermittent memory loss. I...oh. I see he's been assigned to Doctor Webber. I can't do anything without his approval, you understand."

"Is it possible we could speak with Doctor Webber?"

"He's a slippery one," Newman said with a frown. "But we'll give it a go."

He picked up the large black handset from the Dictaphone on his desk and pressed down a lever. "Mrs. Wilson, would you see if you can locate Doctor Webber? I have a couple who...Yes? Oh, would you ask him to step in?" He hung up the phone and grinned. "You're in luck. Usually have a devil of a time getting a hold of him, but he's just gone past. I'd offer you some tea, but I'm afraid we're fresh out at the moment."

"That's all right," Simon said. "We appreciate—"

He was interrupted as the office door opened and a tall, thin disheveled looking man stepped in. He ran a hand through his unruly hair, which proceeded to flop right back into his face. "I was just on my way out, but Ethel said you wanted to see me?"

"Webber, yes, this is Mr. and Mrs. Cross, they've come about one of your patients, Evan Eldridge."

It might have been her imagination, but the mention of Evan's name brought a spark to the doctor's eyes. "Eldridge, Eldridge? Oh, yes, the older gentleman with amnesia, isn't it?"

"He's my uncle," Elizabeth said. "We saw a photograph of him in the paper and we've come an awful long way to take him back home."

"I'm sure you have. He's been a bit of a mystery. No one stepped forward to claim him, until now. No doubt he'll be quite glad to see you. I'm sure we can work something out, but not today, I'm afraid. He's undergone some treatment and won't be quite himself. Tomorrow though. Why don't you come back tomorrow and I'll make sure you're on the list. We'll get started on the paperwork then. We have your details?"

"We're staying over in…" Elizabeth said and then faltered with the name.

"Knightsbridge," Simon provided for her. "It's on the forms."

"I'm sure we can get it all sorted," the doctor said.

"Thank you," Elizabeth said as she got up to shake his hand.

"Oh," he said, obviously surprised at her forwardness. He shook it and then Simon's. "Until tomorrow."

Even though they hadn't actually seen Evan, they'd found him. Elizabeth had repeatedly assured Simon that it would be easy to get Evan and take him home, but part of her hadn't really believed it. Until now. Tomorrow they'd see him and a few days later, take him home.

They left Guy's and walked back across London Bridge. Like most Americans, Elizabeth had always confused London Bridge with Tower Bridge. London Bridge was nice, but it wasn't that quintessential image with the two towers. It was just a bridge. Tower Bridge, not surprisingly had the famous towers and super, olde-Englishy look to it.

From the middle of London Bridge, the Tower Bridge was visible, arching its way over the river. "If we have time," she said, "I'd love to see the Tower of London."

"I'm not sure that's possible. I don't think it's open for tourism. I'm fairly certain it's a working prison right now. Hess was kept there, I think."

She remembered only sketchy details of Rudolf Hess's mysterious flight to Scotland and capture. It was a little creepy to think of Nazi prisoners being held so close to where they were. It was more than likely, she realized, that there were Nazi prisoners all over London.

It was unnerving, but not even the thought of Nazi spies could take her mind off what was important - lunch. It was past noon and the bread and jam they'd eaten that morning had long since worn off. Her stomach grumbled and she idly wondered if she was part Hobbit.

"You know what I'd like to do," she said.

"Buy shoes?"

"Oh, that too, but first, can we get something to eat? I'm starvin' Marvin'."

"Why am I not surprised?" he said as he slipped an arm around her shoulder.

They took the underground from Blackfriars back to South Kensington and started back up toward their flat. They found a small restaurant and had fish pie, which was a bit like shepherd's pie, but with fish instead of beef and Queen cakes, a sort of sponge cake with sultanas mixed in, for dessert. The whole meal cost them one and six, one shilling and sixpence, or about the equivalent of three dollars in modern money.

Filled with fish, they made their way up to Harrod's. In many ways, life seemed so normal. When she focused just on that instant, on the minutia of the moment, it was easy to forget that there was a war on. Then there was a reminder like the pile of rubble of what had once been someone's home or office. Then she remembered that the little brown boxes most people had slung over their shoulders with pieces of string didn't hold lunches, but gasmasks. Even Harrod's was a constant reminder of the war outside.

The store covered an entire block all by itself and, despite the war and shortages, was filled with every good, even if most of the items weren't technically for sale. The shoes she'd picked out, like nearly everything else, could only be bought with ration coupons. They'd managed to bring a book with them, but when push came to shove, Elizabeth couldn't use them. Even in the short time they'd been there, she could see the hardships the people endured. Knowing that the end wasn't as near as they'd hoped, but still three years away, she couldn't bring herself to take what little they had. She'd make do with what she'd brought. The shoes weren't that bad really. She knew she'd get used to them and, in light of what every single person around her was willing to endure, had to endure, it felt like the least she could do.

However, by mid-afternoon, she was pooped. It was kind of embarrassing. They hadn't done much really, but neither of them was used to walking so much. Her aching feet and tired legs were a shameful realization that most of her modern life was spent sitting on her bum. They decided a little rest in their flat was in order before they searched for a place for dinner.

As they climbed the stairs to their room, she felt the fatigue of the long, restless night and the day out finally catching up with her.

Simon keyed open their door and held it open for her.

"I don't know about you," she said, "but I could use a nap."

"Do you mean nap or *nap*?" Simon said with a leer.

Elizabeth walked backwards into the room and ran her hand down Simon's chest as she did. "Maybe we should travel more often."

He followed her in and the door closed behind them. For a moment, they were in pitch black. Then, there was an unexpected click from next to the bed and the room was suddenly illuminated. Elizabeth startled and whirled around, blinking rapidly against the light. When she saw a strange man sitting on the bed, she instinctively stepped back into Simon.

The man had a long scar that ran the length of his cheek and a big black gun in his hand. He stood up and pointed it at them. "Fancy a trip now?"

CHAPTER EIGHT

SIMON'S FIRST INSTINCT WAS to protect Elizabeth and he tried to pull her behind him, but a second man stepped out of the shadows near the door. He grabbed her arm and pulled her out of Simon's grasp.

"Let her go," Simon demanded. His heart and his mind raced. "Who are you? What are you doing here?"

The man by the door made a show of jabbing his gun into Elizabeth's side. The shape of the gun answered Simon's first question—broad grip, long narrow barrel—a Luger. That meant only one thing; they were Germans.

The one with Elizabeth whispered a hushed sibilant shushing sound in her ear that made Elizabeth visibly shiver. Simon's fists clenched with an effort to stay still. He knew he couldn't risk fighting the men. Not both of them. Not here.

"We will be the ones asking the questions," the man with the scar said. "Pray you have the right answers, Professor."

Simon's body tensed as he struggled to keep from moving, his eyes fixed on the gun pressed into Elizabeth's ribs.

"I know you are a smart man, Professor," the man with the scar said.

Professor. That word echoed in Simon's mind and released a torrent of questions. How did they know who he was? What did they want? And, above all else, how could he keep Elizabeth from being hurt?

"You will come with us," the man continued. "And you will not make a scene or my friend will empty his gun into your wife's belly."

Simon ignored the chill that ran through his veins and sought out Elizabeth's eyes across the room. She was frightened, but defiant. He silently begged her to go along and not to struggle. He knew her impulse was to fight back and he knew with equal certainty that she'd die in the trying. *Have faith*, he silently urged her. *We will find a way.*

Simon nodded to the man with the scar. "I understand."

"Very good." He prodded Simon with the gun before slipping it into his pocket. The other man held Elizabeth close and the gun even closer. The four of them left the little flat and made their way downstairs. They passed a couple in the stairwell that simply smiled and bid them a good day.

Every step down the hall and out into the street, Simon looked for an opportunity, but the man held Elizabeth too closely. The four of them walked down the street to a large black sedan. Simon scanned the sidewalk for something, anything that might help them escape, but with the gun digging into Elizabeth's side, there was no move Simon could make that wouldn't risk her life in the bargain.

The one with the gun on Elizabeth opened the back passenger side door. "Get in," he said. "Move over."

"Where are you taking us?" Simon asked.

"What did I say about questions?" the man with the scar said as he nodded to the man in the backseat with Elizabeth. He thrust the gun into Elizabeth's ribs and she arched away from him and grimaced in pain.

"Don't," Simon pleaded.

Elizabeth caught Simon's eyes and tried to assure him she was all right. She wasn't. Nothing about this was all right.

"Get in."

Simon gripped the edge of the car door and got into the passenger seat. The man with the scar got behind the wheel. He turned to Simon. "If you try anything clever, my friend will kill your wife. Do we understand each other?"

"Yes," Simon said and looked back to see the man in the back seat put one arm around Elizabeth's shoulder with his gun-hand pressed into her side. He tried to calm his racing heart and clear his head. He couldn't let his rage take control of him. These men wanted something, something from him, but what could it possibly be? No one here knew who they really were. They'd been here less than a day; they hadn't seen anything they shouldn't have. He hoped it was all a mistake, a horrible mistake. That thought didn't hold much comfort though. If anything, it was worse. Mistake or not, these men had no intention of letting them go. They hadn't hidden their faces nor had they bothered to blindfold them. It was painfully clear that these men had no intention of letting them out of this alive. Simon could only hope whatever these thugs needed him for gave him some leverage or bought him sufficient time so he could find a way to save Elizabeth and himself.

They drove for another ten minutes before the car turned off into an alley. Simon didn't know the exact streets they'd taken, but he knew they were somewhere in Camden. They got out of the car and the gunmen led them down the alley.

Simon and Elizabeth's eyes met again. Neither needed words to say what they were feeling. She was frightened, but she was ready to follow his lead. It was clear she understood as well as he did that the only escape from this would be one of their own making. Simon tried to silently assure her he'd find a way, when the man holding her jerked to a stop.

One of the men unlocked a heavy metal door and forced them inside. The man with the scar flipped on a light. They were in what looked like a storage room for some sort of music store. Crates of records and a few instruments were piled along the walls.

He led them through the storage room and into a dark hall where he opened another door. He turned on the light and gestured for Simon to go first. Simon turned back to check on Elizabeth. The man held her tightly, gun still pressed into her side. Simon clenched his jaw and. with little other choice, went through the door. It led to a rickety wooden staircase to the basement. He heard Elizabeth and the other man follow him down the stairs. The basement was large and mostly empty. A few crates were stacked along the walls and two chairs sat alone in the middle of the room, one tipped on its side. A single bare light bulb dangled from a ceiling chain.

When Simon reached the bottom of the stairs, he turned around. For a brief moment it was just the three of them. The man with the scar was still upstairs. He could tell from her expression that Elizabeth realized it too and her eyes took on a wide-eyed urgency. If they were going to move against the gunmen, now was the time.

The sound of a Glenn Miller record playing upstairs filtered down to them. The other man must have put on a record to muffle the sounds that would come from the basement. The sounds of their cries of anguish. Simon could not let that happen. The music distracted the man with the gun on Elizabeth.

This was Simon's opportunity. He'd been plotting this moment in his head since they'd been taken from their room. First, a sharp blow to the temple to stun him and get control of the weapon. Second, a jab to the larynx to silence him. And, third, whatever the hell had to do to get Elizabeth out alive.

The man took his eyes off them and looked up the stairs. As he turned, the gun pivoted away from Elizabeth's side.

Simon's hand clenched into a fist. He started to lunge.

"I wouldn't do that if I were you."

Simon whipped his head around and saw the man with the scar standing at the top of the stairs, his gun trained on Elizabeth. He'd been too slow and it had cost them their chance. With a grunt Simon stepped back and caught Elizabeth's eyes. They both knew the moment and quite possibly their one chance at escape had come and gone.

"Idiot," the man with the scar said to the other as he tossed him a few lengths of rope. "Tie them up."

He kept his gun trained on Elizabeth as his partner picked up the toppled wooden chair and positioned it back to back with the other. He moved the chairs so that they were about two feet apart and facing away from each other. The man with the scar motioned for Simon and Elizabeth to sit down and his partner bound Simon's hands to the wooden slats and then added ropes around his waist and ankles to secure him to the chair. As the minutes ticked past, Simon could do nothing but sit helplessly by. His hands strained against the bonds as he tried vainly to reach Elizabeth, to touch her. She was only a few feet away, but it felt like so much more.

The worst part though, was not being able to see her anymore. If he could just see her…He tried to turn his head to catch a glimpse of her, but one of the men shoved his head back around. Once they were sure the ropes were secure, the man with the scar casually walked around to stand in front of Simon. He smiled down at him, but there was no kindness in it. This man was ruthless and took joy in it.

Music filtered down from upstairs. A pulsing big band song filled with the rhythms of life made a strange counterpoint to the slow methodical cruelty below.

Simon strained vainly against the ropes that bound him. He'd brought Elizabeth to England to ask her to spend the rest of her life with him. A rich, full life. It would not end this way, he vowed. These men would not take her from him. Not here. Not today.

The man with the scar placed a foot on one of the crates, lit a cigarette and leaned forward, casually resting an elbow on his knee. He took a deep drag off his cigarette and then exhaled slowly.

"You've made a mistake," Simon said. "We're not whomever you think we are."

"No?"

"Let us go and we promise not to say anything about this," Elizabeth said.

Simon heard the defiance and the fear in her voice. The man with the scar just laughed. Simon knew what that laughter meant. He closed his eyes and tried to calm himself. His only weapon was his mind. Maybe he could negotiate with them. He seemed to be their target.

"Let her go. You can keep me," Simon said. He was desperate to find some way, any way to get Elizabeth out of there. "I'll do whatever you ask, if you let her go."

"Simon—"

"I could help you," Simon offered. He tried to keep his voice calm. "I don't know what you need, but I'm not without resources. But I'll only help you, if you let her go."

"I think it is the other way around," the leader said. "You will help me *because* she is here."

And then all Simon heard was the whip-crack of the man's palm as it connected with Elizabeth's face. She gasped and he could hear her swallow her cry of pain.

"No!" Simon said.

Simon tried to reach out and strangle the man smiling back at him, but the ropes cut into his wrists and the tethers on his rage were tested. His hands shook with the force of his effort, but the bindings were too tight. When he was free of them, he was going to make them both pay for that. He would beat them to a bloody pulp with his bare hands.

He heard Elizabeth take in a deep, unsteady breath. "I'm okay."

The defiance in her voice made his heart ache and swell.

The man with the scar casually waved his gun toward Elizabeth. "Your wife is a lovely woman, Professor Cross. It would be a shame if anything ruined that." He put the gun down on a crate. The ball of fear in Simon's stomach was suddenly electrified.

"Guns are so messy, so indelicate. So quick."

It was just a few feet away. So damn tantalizingly close. If Simon could just reach it.

Then the man pulled out a switchblade and flicked it open. He cut the air with the knife. "Knives are a tool for the artist." He motioned for the other man to come to him. He handed him the knife and the man grinned.

"Alas, my friend is no artist. He's clumsy. Too bad for your wife."

The man took the knife behind Simon to Elizabeth. Simon's entire body was on fire. "Elizabeth!"

He struggled against the ropes, cursing every moment that had led them to this. If his will alone were a weapon, both men would have dropped dead on the spot. Simon raged against the helplessness and fixated on how he would exact his revenge. If they touched her...

"Don't listen to him, Simon."

"Cut out her tongue."

"No!" Simon roared. Simon squeezed his eyes shut to wipe out the image from this mind. "Please. What do you want from me?"

The man with the scar waved for his partner to stop. "Now that we have an understanding, we can begin in earnest. Who do you work for?"

Simon stuck with their script. If he could get them to just tell him what they wanted, he could come up with a way to deal with them. "I work for the United States government. I do research in alternative materials."

"Don't tell them anything!" Elizabeth cried.

"Elizabeth, please."

"You should listen to your husband. But then most wives don't, do they? I know mine doesn't."

He smiled at Simon as if they shared some common kinship. It made Simon sick to his stomach.

"We're here on family business," Simon said. "It's got nothing to do with the war."

The man with the scar leaned back. "Everything has to do with the war."

"Not this. We're just here to take her uncle home."

The smile faded from the man's face. "Do not play games with me. What do you know about the Shard? Do you know where it is?"

The Shard. Simon's mind raced for something, anything to latch onto, but there was nothing. He'd never heard of any Shard. He wished to God he had. He'd tell them anything they wanted to know if it meant saving Elizabeth. "I don't know what you're talking about."

The man with the scar nodded to his partner. Before Simon could protest he heard the horrible sound of another slap. Simon tried to lunge out of his chair, but the ropes held him back. His chair rocked forward and then fell back into position. His arms strained against his restraints. The only thing he wanted in the world at that moment was to burst free and strangle them both with the ropes they'd used to bind him.

"I am not a patient man. But I will ask you again. What do you know about the Shard?"

Simon tried to think of something, anything to buy time, anything to keep the focus on him and not Elizabeth. He wracked his brain for any mention of a shard in history. "The Shard," he repeated. "Maybe if you can tell me—"

Suddenly, the music stopped. Simon and the man with the scar looked toward the top of the stairs. Someone else was there. Please, dear God, let them be on our side, Simon thought.

The man with the scar picked up his gun and motioned for his partner to stay put. Slowly, he started up the stairs. The door to the hallway burst open and a gunshot rang out. Simon ducked reflexively, but ropes held him in place. The man with the scar grunted and stumbled back down a few stairs. He clutched his shoulder; blood seeped from the wound and stained the white of his shirt beneath his jacket. He returned fire as he retreated back into the basement.

It was deafening. In the small room each gunshot was an explosion of sound. Elizabeth screamed and Simon tried to turn to her. The other man yelled something in German. Bullets ricocheted off the brick walls. Each strike exploded the brick into tiny pieces that rained down onto the floor like crackling hail. A bullet buried itself into the crate near Simon with a whump. More shots were fired and Elizabeth screamed again.

"Elizabeth!"

In the midst of the madness, Simon rocked his chair and tried to move it toward her when more gunshots cracked from the top of the stairs. Whoever was up there had better cover and pressed his advantage. The wounded gunman edged along the brick wall toward another doorway in the corner of the basement. He yelled something in German, fired again and opened the door.

The man on the stairs inched his way down, gun at the ready. When he came into the light Simon saw that it was the American from the Ritz, Jack Wells. They caught each other's eyes briefly and Wells was as surprised as he was.

"Look out!" Elizabeth shouted.

Wells ducked just in time. The bullet hit the wall above his shoulder. Then, Simon heard a grunt of pain coming from behind him. Wells fired in the direction of the sound, over Simon's head. Another gasp quickly followed, and then the sound of a man falling to the floor.

"Elizabeth?" Simon said. "Are you hurt?" He managed to turn his chair enough so that he could see her.

"I'm okay," she said.

Wells dashed toward the doorway the German had fled through and ran out after him.

"Are you sure?" Simon said twisting against the ropes.

Elizabeth nodded. "Yeah. You?"

"Damn these ropes," Simon said as he strained against them.

Wells reappeared in the doorway and stuffed his gun into his shoulder holster. "Funny meeting you two here."

"For God's sake untie us," Simon said.

As soon as Simon was free he moved to Elizabeth's side, nearly tripping over the dead man on the floor at her feet. He quickly surveyed her for injuries, and aside from a bright red cheek, she looked unharmed. "Are you sure you're all right?"

She nodded, but kept staring down at the dead man. Blood oozed out into a deep red puddle beneath the body. Simon gently tilted her head so that he could see into her eyes. He knew what she was feeling. He was feeling it too—anger, confusion and shock. He said her name again and she broke out of the daze.

"Thanks for that," Wells said with a grin, nodding toward the body.

"For what?" Simon asked.

Wells smiled. "He was just about to plug me when she, uhm, kicked him in the fatherland."

Elizabeth shrugged demurely. Simon smiled inwardly; that was his girl. She laughed nervously. "Score one for Uncle Sam."

Simon knew the bravado wasn't real. He could hear the tremor in her voice.

"Come on, let's get out of here." Wells slipped the dead man's gun into his pocket and gestured toward the stairs.

"Who *are* you?" Simon demanded as he helped Elizabeth toward the stairs. "And what the devil was that all about?"

"Hell on earth, Mr. Cross," Wells said. "Hell on earth."

CHAPTER NINE

SIMON, ELIZABETH AND WELLS left the music store through the storeroom and the alley door. Simon kept a tight hold on Elizabeth's hand, mostly to make sure no one could take her from him, but partly to stop his own from shaking. They were safe, for now, but the worst could have happened. Would have happened if it hadn't been for Wells. They passed the German's car and Elizabeth abruptly stopped and ran toward it.

"What on earth are you doing?" Simon said.

She opened the back door and reached in for something. She held up her prize. "My purse!"

Simon stared at her incredulously.

"What?" she said as she hurried back to his side. "It's got all of my papers and half of our money."

"Women," Jack said. "Come on." He got into a brown sedan and reached back to open the suicide door to the backseat for them.

Simon hesitated before getting into Wells' car, but at this point he had to trust the man, at least enough to get them away from this damned place. He let Elizabeth get into the car and slid in after her. Wells sped away into traffic.

"Were those two Nazis?" Elizabeth asked.

"They weren't Sunshine Girls," Jack said.

Simon examined Elizabeth's cheek as she chattered on nervously. It didn't appear to be too injured, but it was beginning to swell.

"Yeah, I guess not. Wow. Am I talking really loud? I think I am, but I can't tell. My ears are ringing."

"It'll get better in a few minutes," Jack said loudly.

Simon took Elizabeth's hand and squeezed it. He couldn't quite get past how close he'd come to losing her and, despite her bravado, he could tell she felt it too. His worry and love for her was raw and exposed. It left him feeling angry and vulnerable. He saw Wells' eyes on them in the rearview mirror.

"Who the hell *are* you?" Simon asked.

Jack laughed. "I was just wondering the same thing about you."

Simon hardly felt there was anything funny about what had just happened. He was about to point that out to Wells when Elizabeth spoke.

"Simon," she said. "He did just save our lives."

Simon grunted, but had to agree on that point. "Yes, thank you."

"How did you know we were there?" Elizabeth asked.

"I didn't. I've been keeping tabs on Hans and Otto for a few months now. I got wind that somebody had gotten into the car with them, extra chummy-like, you know? So, I headed over to the music store as fast as I could. I figured they weren't planning a spring social."

Wells' behavior at the Ritz with King Zog, his knowledge of politics and languages started to make sense. Combine that with this afternoon and Simon realized who Wells was. A spy. 1942 was too early for the CIA. It was formed after the war. "You're with the OSS."

Jack stared at him in the mirror, eyes narrowed. "Not for long, if crap like this keeps happening."

"Did I mention wow?" Elizabeth said.

"How did they know about us, about where we're staying?" Simon asked. That point had been particularly troubling. "We've only just arrived in town and the only people we've met were the hospital staff and you."

Wells held up a hand in surrender. "I didn't know anything about your connection to all of this until I saw you in the basement."

Wells had looked surprised to find them there, but it was still more coincidental than Simon was comfortable with, not that he was in any position to cast stones at the moment. For now, he was grateful whatever the reason.

"I'll get you a room at St. Ermin's with me," Wells said as he drove them back toward the city's center. "The manager owes me a favor."

"What about our things?" Elizabeth asked Simon. "They're still at the apartment."

"Nothing we can't do without."

She looked at him questioningly and Simon opened his jacket, reached into his pocket and showed her the watch was safely in his possession. She reached for the silver necklace Teddy Fiske had given her. She felt along the strand until she came to the small key.

She smiled back at him and took his hand. "I guess we've got everything that matters."

Wells drove them to his hotel, the Jolly Hotel St. Ermin's, an enormous and elegant old building with Victorian flair in the heart of Westminster. As they walked into a lobby filled with men in uniforms, Simon had a flash of recognition and realized the significance. St. Ermin's had been the home of many of Churchill's most important meetings. The SOE, MI6 and God knew who else were headquartered there during the war. Even the infamous

Cambridge five of *Tinker, Tailor, Soldier, Spy* fame had used it for some of their clandestine exchanges.

Wells' suite wasn't the biggest the hotel had to offer, but still impressive. The sitting room itself was twice the size of their little flat.

"This is nice," Elizabeth said as she admired the upscale furnishings.

"Yeah, pretty posh, isn't it? A friend got transferred back to the States. I just sort of took over the lease," Wells said as he tossed his jacket onto a chair and loosened his tie. "Make yourselves comfortable."

He turned on an enormous wireless radio and spun the dial until he stopped on a channel playing Benny Goodman. Then he picked up the phone and tapped the cradle down a few times to reach the operator. "Room service."

Despite the fact that Wells had saved their lives, Simon wasn't about to relax. Adrenaline still pulsed through his body. He'd come so close to losing her, too damn close. She picked at a corner of one of the pillows on the sofa, wrapping a lose thread around her finger again and again.

"Are you all right?" he asked her.

"Stop worrying. I'm fine."

She wasn't. Hell, he wasn't either. After what they'd just been through, she'd be lucky if he ever let her out of his sight again. "We should ice your cheek."

"I doubt this place has a minibar." She was right, of course.

"Bathroom?" he asked Wells who pointed down the hall. "Ice?"

Wells nodded and ordered sandwiches and a bucket of ice.

They found the bath and Simon busied himself preparing a cold washcloth while Elizabeth examined her face in the mirror. His hands shook and he gripped the edges of the sink for a moment. He hadn't felt this helpless since King Kashian. He pushed the sickening memory away, picked up the cold cloth and placed it against her cheek.

"I'm sorry," he said softly. It wasn't enough. He should have been able to find a way to protect her.

"It's not too bad. Let's hope all Nazis hit like girls."

"Elizabeth—"

"Don't," she said. Fear and despair briefly crossed her face before she chased them away. "We made it. That's what counts, right?"

It mattered more than he could possibly express. He could spend a lifetime trying to explain how much she meant to him and never come close. "I don't know what I'd do if I lost you."

Elizabeth's chin wobbled and she looked up at him, eyes wet with unshed tears. Maybe love didn't always need words.

After a moment, Elizabeth grabbed some tissue and wiped her eyes. "We should get back. Don't want Jack to think we're doing strange things in his bathroom."

Simon held her arm. Wells had saved their lives, but there was no way to know what his end game was. "Can we trust him?"

"Can we really afford not to?"

It was a Hobson's choice. Trust a man he didn't know or trust no one. Considering their circumstances, he'd have to trust Wells. A little.

They rejoined Jack in the sitting area. "Everything okay?"

Elizabeth nodded. "Now, about those Nazis. "

"Technically, they're SS," Wells said. "Himmler's own."

Simon looked to the heavens. Wonderful. They'd somehow managed not just to get involved in something dangerous, but something that involved the bloody SS. The sooner they got out of the country the better.

Wells gestured for them to sit down. "Why don't we start with you telling me just what this family business is you're here for?"

Simon and Elizabeth exchanged uncomfortable glances as they sat down. No matter who this man was they could never tell him the real truth. Of course, Simon was fairly certain that cut both ways.

"Look," Wells said. "I'm one of the good guys. I'd hope saving your lives might have earned me a little trust."

Elizabeth cast a quick glance at Simon. "We do trust you."

Wells gave Simon an appraising look. Gone was the easy-going adventurer from the Ritz. These were the eyes of a keen observer and shrewd judge. He took full stock of Simon, of his anger, his fear, and his suspicion in a matter of seconds and smiled. It was wholly discomfiting to be read so quickly and so clearly.

"Good," Jack said.

Simon shifted in his seat and let out a breath. "They asked me about some sort of shard." He hoped to redirect the conversation away from their reasons for being there and back to why someone had nearly killed them.

"And you don't know what that is?" Wells asked skeptically.

"No idea," Simon said. "But after our...experience this afternoon, I'd very much like to."

Wells studied them carefully and then cocked his head to the side. "You're either two of the best liars I've ever seen or you really don't know what's going on."

"We're terrible liars," Elizabeth said. "Especially me."

Wells chuckled. "That I believe."

"What *is* going on?" Simon asked.

Wells considered that for a moment, lit a cigarette and offered them one. They both declined and he took a deep drag before he started. "About three months ago two Swiss agents turned up dead just outside of Swindon. Ends up they're transporting something important, some sort of artifact. Supposedly, they were there to make a deal with someone. We don't know if it was the Germans or someone else, but whatever the plan was it didn't work out and they got themselves killed. And the artifact turned up missing."

"The Shard."

"Right. And the last man to see them alive was your friend, Evan Eldridge."

"Uncle." Elizabeth corrected him. "How is he involved?"

"I was hoping you could tell me. When MI5 finally found him, he was near dead, probably should have been. Got cracked on the head pretty good. When he finally came to, he had no idea where he was or what he was doing there. They took him away and have been trying to get information out of him ever since, but he kind of comes and goes. Just about every spy service in London has been waiting for months for someone to make contact with him."

"And we did yesterday," Simon said. At least part of the puzzle was fitting together. "But what's the shard? Why is it so important?"

"This is gonna sound a little nutty, but have you ever heard of Nothung?"

"Nothing?" Elizabeth said.

"No, Nothung."

"Who's on first?"

"What?"

"Elizabeth," Simon chided before she continued with the entire Abbot and Costello routine. He knew it was nerves, and he hardly blamed her, but details of the shard were important.

She had the good sense to look chagrined. "Sorry."

"I mean the sword," Wells said. "From the opera, ya know?"

"*Der Ring des Nibelungen*," Simon said. That did not bode well. "Wagner."

"Yeah, well, it's real or at least the Germans think so. And they're pretty hell-bent on finding all the pieces."

"Pieces?" Elizabeth said. "I don't understand."

"The shard," Simon said as he worked it through. "In the story, Siegfried is given the shards of his father's sword, Nothung or Gram or Balmung. It goes by many names."

Simon couldn't think sitting down and got up to pace the length of the room. "The opera is based on several different stories—folktales and Norse legends—but basically it tells the story of a man, Siegfried, who is on a quest to destroy a dragon with the sword and find a ring that will give him dominion over the earth."

"Like the One Ring in Tolkien."

"A bit, yes. There are some similarities. But Wagner's version is, by many accounts, frighteningly anti-Semitic and ultimately a parable for the ascension of the Arian race to its preordained status as Gods among men."

The distaste on Elizabeth's face mirrored his feelings exactly.

Simon nodded in agreement and continued. "The idea is that Siegfried, with the re-forged fragments of his father's sword, can defeat the mighty dragon, seize the ring and rule the world. Substitute Hitler for Siegfried and, well, you get the picture."

"That about sums it up," Wells said.

Elizabeth tucked her feet under her, a sure sign they were in for the long haul. "Shouldn't we be worried about the ring and not the sword?"

Simon considered that. "Without the sword he can't win the ring. And there have been references to the sword specifically through the centuries in several texts. Primarily Austrian and Scandinavian. Supposedly, it was shattered in battle and the pieces spread across the land. Of course, I've never actually seen the codices myself."

Wells, who'd been conspicuously quiet, stubbed out his cigarette. His hand edged closer to the gun hanging from his shoulder holster. "You know an awful lot about this stuff. How is that?"

Wells had been testing them and it looked like a passing grade might have been worse than failing. There was no backing away from it now. "I'm a professor of the Occult. I've studied these legends for most of my life."

"And you're being here now is just coincidence, huh?"

"As absurd as that sounds," Simon said. "Yes."

Wells leaned forward and regarded them skeptically. "No offense, but I'm finding that a bit hard to swallow."

"If I'd known what Eldridge was involved in, what the dangers were, do you think I would have risked Elizabeth's life?"

Wells narrowed his eyes, unconvinced.

Simon looked at Elizabeth. Without taking his eyes off her he continued. "Have you ever been in love Mr. Wells?"

"War changes things."

"Not everything, Mr. Wells. Not everything."

"All right," Wells said. "Suppose I believe you. About the sword. I'm just a guy from the streets of Chicago. We don't have magical swords where I come from. Do you really believe this mumbo-jumbo?"

It was horrifying to consider. If Nothung were real, if the legends were true..."It really isn't important if I believe it, is it?"

"No," Wells agreed. "Even if the damn thing is just a sword, if *they* believe it, if the German people believe it's real...Give zealots something to latch onto and—" He was interrupted by a knock on the door.

Simon instinctively reached for Elizabeth and started to stand.

Wells motioned for him to stay where he was and un-holstered his gun. Why did everyone in this blasted city have a gun but him?

"Who is it?" Wells said as he went to the door.

"Room service."

He cracked the door a few inches before shouldering his gun and opening it the rest of the way. Simon relaxed back into his seat.

Wells took the tray from the young attendant. "Cross? You want to…?" he nodded toward the boy and his outstretched hand.

Cheeky. Simon dug a few coins out of his pocket, tipped the boy and closed the door. Wells set down the tray of sandwiches and took a few handfuls of ice from the ice bucket. He put them into a towel, tied it up like a hobo's bag and handed it to Elizabeth. "They were out of steak. Rations."

Wells drank down half a glass of beer and frowned. "I hate English beer."

Elizabeth pressed the ice-bag to the side of her face and winced. Despite that, she reached for a sandwich that seemed to distract her from the pain.

Wells picked up a sandwich and took a bite. "A lot of good men," he said with his mouth full, "died letting us know the Germans have the rest of the sword. Now, everybody wants the last shard. Of course, we Americans think it would be safest in our hands."

Elizabeth nodded, her mouth full. Simon shook his head and she shrugged. "Danger makes me hungry."

"The only lead any of us have is Evan Eldridge, who can't or won't talk." Wells finished his sandwich. "And then came you."

"But we don't have anything to do with it," Elizabeth said.

"You do now."

Chapter Ten

Elizabeth watched Simon pace across the floor of their hotel room. "Trust him, he says."

True to his word, Jack arranged a room down the hall from his. It wasn't a suite, but it was a definite improvement over their room at the B&B. No more freezing cold trips down the hall in the middle of the night. And, hopefully no Nazis.

"Well, he did save our lives."

Simon looked at his watch. "We'll give it another few minutes."

"And then?" Elizabeth said with more bite than she'd meant. She'd anticipated this conversation and dreaded having it. Her nerves were so frayed around the edges, one tug and she was sure she would unravel.

"Leave. Leave this hotel, leave this city."

"We can't do that."

"Of course we can. Or have you forgotten that we were nearly killed an hour ago?"

She held up the ice bag. That seemed to suitably chasten him. "I'm sorry."

"Don't be." She knew, as ridiculous as it was, he blamed himself for what happened to them. Simon still wore the world, at least her part of it, on his shoulders. She got up from the bed and took his hands in hers. "And what you said—"

"Nothing's worth your life."

That wasn't true and they both knew it. Jack was right. War did change things. Now that they were in the middle of it and not just on the sidelines, Elizabeth felt that truth for the first time and it made her feel slightly queasy. The weight of what was at stake pressed down on her.

"We shouldn't interfere," Simon said.

"Maybe that's why Evan was here. What if something changed and he was here to set it right?"

"Pure conjecture." Simon waved it away. She'd expected him to and didn't take it personally, but she was tired and didn't have the energy to fight. "Right. We're guessing."

She let go of Simon's hands and walked away, rubbing her hands up and down her arms. "And we'll never know for sure unless we talk to Evan."

"It's too dangerous."

Elizabeth leaned against the bathroom doorway and wrapped her arms around her chest. "Running around the countryside with the Nazis on our trail doesn't sound like a picnic. At least here we've got an ally."

"But can we really trust him?" Simon said as he moved in front of her. "All we have is his word?"

"And that's all he has from us. Not to mention the fact that he's come to our rescue not once, but twice. I think he's earned our trust."

Simon sighed, resigned to it. "For now."

Elizabeth stepped forward and put her arms around his waist. She was happy to concede the nuance of that point. "For now."

Simon's eyes softened and he lightly touched her cheek. "Does it hurt?"

With a swiftness that surprised her, her throat tightened and tears welled in her eyes. She held back the tidal wave of emotion and managed a weak smile. "Only when I'm kissed senseless. But I hear it's worth it."

Simon kissed her gently. When he pulled away she could see the worry in his eyes. It was too much. The hold she had on her emotions slipped for only a moment, but that was all it took. The pressure was too great.

Not wanting to fall to pieces in front him, she kept her eyes down and patted his chest. "I'm gonna wash up."

Elizabeth slipped into the bathroom and closed the door behind her. She turned on the cold-water tap and caught a glimpse of herself in the mirror. Her hair was a mess; her lipstick smudged like a crazy woman's and her cheek was bright red. She looked ridiculous. A slightly hysterical laugh bubbled up in her throat, but by the time it came out it was a soft sob. She'd managed not to cry all afternoon, but there was no escaping it now. She blew out a shaky breath and tried to calm her frayed nerves.

She'd never been hit like that before. Unable to defend herself, unable to help Simon. The stakes had never been so high before. The reality of everything that happened that afternoon crashed down on her.

Her brave face had finally cracked and it felt good to let go. The tears came and she didn't fight them. Was she really strong enough to do this? To fight the Nazis?

She wasn't Oskar Schindler or Audie Murphy or any of the others who risked their lives a dozen times over.

It was a strange and painful realization to now understand so keenly that all of those people weren't characters in a movie or a book; they were real people, living now, fighting now, and dying now. She'd always prided herself on being someone who did the right thing, who was willing to help.

This was her chance. Was she brave enough to do what needed to be done? Her reflection, tear stained and puffy eyed looked back at her. It was one of those rare moments of complete self-honesty. A moment where she saw into herself and knew the answer. She would never be able to look herself in the eyes again if she didn't at least try.

Simon knocked on the door. "All right in there?"

Elizabeth sniffed and wiped at her eyes. "Yes."

Simon opened the door and peeked in. She splashed cold water on her face and dabbed it dry with a towel.

She could tell from the expression on his face that he could see she'd been crying. It was the last thing she wanted. She knew if he saw her this way, it would fuel his argument to leave. It was a fight she didn't want to have.

She smiled and tried to pretend that she'd just been washing her face even though they both knew it was a lie. "That felt good."

Simon didn't say anything for a moment, then took the damp towel from her hand and laid it on the sink's edge. "You don't ever have to hide from me."

"I know." It was embarrassing to be so transparent. She felt the tears pricking at her eyes again.

Simon tilted her head up. "Do you?"

Simon's eyes were filled with understanding, empathy and love. In all her life, she'd never felt completely and utterly accepted before. But in that moment, in that instant looking into Simon's eyes, she was.

Elizabeth slept better than she'd expected. Nightmares had come and gone, but Simon was constant, warm, and reassuring enough to ease her back into sleep. While she wasn't exactly feeling peppy, she felt stronger today and was ready to move forward. Wherever that led them. They would face it together. And in clean clothes.

In addition to their freshly laundered clothes and new hat for Simon, another package arrived. Simon kissed her and opened it. "Clean smalls." He pulled out a pair of panties and dangled them in the air. "And just how does he know your size?"

Elizabeth snatched them out of his hand and picked up a pair of boxers. "I could be asking you the same question."

They dressed and headed downstairs. There was a note from Jack at the desk. They shouldn't have any trouble getting in to see Evan and he'd meet them for a late lunch at the hotel. And, just to play it safe, he'd arranged for a car to take them to and from the hospital.

Whatever arrangements he'd made cut right through the red tape that had bound them the day before and they were ushered into a vacant day room to wait for Evan. Restless, Elizabeth explored the room. There wasn't much to see. Hospital white walls and hospital white floors. She idly played with a shape puzzle, trying to see if she could put a square peg in a round hole when the door opened.

Her puzzle forgotten, Elizabeth looked up and her breath caught in her throat. Eldridge looked very little like the vibrant, warm man she'd seen so many times in his portrait. This man appeared ten years older and sat hunched over in a wheelchair, his silver hair too long and his face drawn and pale.

"You have five minutes," the nurse said.

"Can't we have longer?" Elizabeth asked. She hadn't expected so little time.

"Five minutes."

The nurse left, but Evan gave no notice of it. He stayed head hung down, hands in his lap.

Elizabeth looked nervously toward Simon who silently urged her on.

"Uncle Evan?"

Nothing.

Slowly, she moved closer, pulling a chair next his. "Uncle Evan, we're here to take you home. To San Francisco."

For the first time, he raised his head. His eyes were bloodshot, but they weren't unfocused. "Are you...?"

"Yes, Lillian misses you very much."

At the mention of her name, his eyes moistened. He reached out and Elizabeth grasped his hand. It was cold and frail.

"Am I dreaming? I can't tell anymore."

Elizabeth's heart ached for him. "No, you're not dreaming. We're going to take you back home. Aunt Lillian misses you very much. We all do. Teddy and Max and me."

His eyes searched her face for any glimmer of something familiar. She'd been so struck by the way the artist had captured his eyes in the painting. They'd been so filled with kindness and understanding. It was disconcerting to see them so lost and afraid now.

"So far away," he said with a shake of his head.

He was barely lucid. There was one thing left to try.

"How much longer?" Elizabeth asked Simon who, as planned, made a show of taking out the watch to check.

"Just a few more minutes," he said, showing her, and Evan the watch.

She thought she saw Evan's eyes flash for a brief moment, but she wasn't sure. His gaze turned to her and his eyes searched her face for something and then he drifted off. "It's like swimming in soup. A nice split-pea."

Elizabeth's heart sank. They weren't going to get any information out of him. All they could do was reassure him and, God willing, get him out of here.

"Perhaps they're giving him drugs," Simon said.

Evan looked up at Simon and smiled dreamily. "Oh, yes, delightful pills. So pretty." Very subtly, he tugged on Elizabeth's hand. "Like you, my dear."

She moved in to accept a kiss on the cheek.

In a voice so quiet she had to strain to hear him, Evan whispered in her ear. "They're watching us. Forget me, get the Shard and destroy it."

He leaned back and his gaze danced aimlessly along the ceiling. "Just lovely."

Elizabeth did her best to remain outwardly calm. "It's so good to see you, Uncle. We've been terribly worried about you."

"As you can see, I'm perfectly fine," he said in a quiet, dreamy voice.

"Yes, I can see that they've taken very good care of you," Simon said.

"Oh, yes," Evan said nodding his head slowly. "Very good."

The door to the hall opened and the nurse stepped in. "Time's up."

Elizabeth was about to argue that it had hardly been five minutes, but knew it would do no good. She squeezed Evan's hand. "We'll come back tomorrow. You're going home." She leaned forward and hugged him.

"Charing Cross," he whispered. "Iona by Gaspar. Destroy it. Don't come back here; it's too dangerous." He pulled her closer and kissed her cheek. "Tell Lilly that I love her and that I'm sorry." Then he settled listlessly back into his chair.

"We'll see you tomorrow, Uncle," Elizabeth said, barely holding back the torrent of emotions raging inside her. "I promise."

As the nurse wheeled him out of the room, he got the same faraway look he had when they'd brought him in. "Could I have some soup, do you think? A nice split-pea."

The exchange unnerved Elizabeth and it took her a moment to plaster a smile back on her face. The fervor in his voice was terrifying, and the sadness so haunting.

Dr. Webber, the one in charge of Evan's care, appeared in the doorway. He leaned into the room. "I'd heard you were here. Everything go all right?"

"Yes," Elizabeth said. "Thank you. Everything went very well."

The ride back to the hotel was silent. They'd have to be careful what they said and where they said it, from here on out. The walls everywhere could have ears and eyes.

They started into the hotel, but Elizabeth took Simon by the hand. "How about a walk? Maybe there's a park close by? I could use some fresh air."

"St. James isn't far."

It wasn't. After just a few blocks they were at the park's edge.

"It's so strange to see it without fences," Simon said.

The park was beautiful and the fall air was crisp, but not too cold. They found a bench along a path on the edge of the lake. Ducks gathered on the near shore and half a dozen barrage balloons hung in the sky above the city in the distance.

Elizabeth told Simon everything that Evan had said and she wasn't surprised that he was less than pleased with her promise.

"You've got to stop doing that," he said. "Making promises we can't keep."

She'd thought long and hard about this on the way back from the hospital. Although, if she were honest with herself, she'd known from the start where she stood. No matter how shaky the ground.

"Why can't we?"

"Elizabeth—"

"If you could have heard him. Heard the urgency in his voice. Simon, he's willing to sacrifice himself so that we can get the Shard. Or at least so we can try."

"Try what? To find a mythical artifact that may or may not be hidden somewhere in England?"

Elizabeth heard the frustration in Simon's voice and tried not to echo it. "Not just somewhere. Charing Cross Road. And yesterday you seemed pretty sure it wasn't mythical."

"That was before we were racing Nazis to find it." He shook his head.

She nudged closer so she could lower her voice. "Does Iona by Gaspar mean anything to you?"

"No. It could be anything. A painting, a song…"

Elizabeth noticed a young woman sitting under a tree reading. "Or a book."

Simon frowned in thought. "Charing Cross does have quite a few antiquarian bookshops."

Any lead was a welcome one and Elizabeth leapt at this one. "Sounds like a good place to start."

Simon leaned away from her so he could get a good look into her eyes. "Are you sure you want to do this?"

They'd been down this road. She shook her head with resignation. "Can we really afford not to? What if it is as powerful as they think it is and it falls into the wrong hands?

Simon had no answer for that.

Elizabeth looked off into the distance. "Jack was right. War changes everything."

CHAPTER ELEVEN

JACK WAS WAITING FOR them in the hotel lobby. He stood as he saw them enter and waved them over. "Was starting to get worried. Everything go okay?"

"Yes," Simon said. "Sorry, we went for a short walk. Thank you for the driver."

"You're welcome. Must have been quite a parade. You picked up a pretty long tail."

They had a tail? "We did?" Elizabeth said far too loudly as she looked anxiously around.

Jack laughed. "Subtle."

"Do you mean we were followed?" Simon asked.

"Yup."

Elizabeth looked around a little more surreptitiously this time. She scanned the faces and the clothes carefully. "Are they watching us right now?"

"You two really are greenhorns, aren't you? Come on, let's get some grub and we'll bring each other up to speed."

The restaurant at St. Ermin's was as elegant as the rest of the hotel. Silver service and white table clothes were a strange counterpoint to the grays and privation she knew were just outside.

Jack found them a corner table and the waiter came by with menus. It wasn't expansive and, honestly, she had no idea what most of it was. Why did the English call every dessert pudding even when it wasn't? She gave Simon a look of distress that signaled, order for me or I'll end up with tripe again. She and her stomach were still trying to forget that night.

England, being an island and the last hold out against the Axis powers in Europe, was severely cut off from supplies. America sent what it could, but the basics—eggs, milk, meat, butter—were scarce and heavily rationed. Anyone who cooked at home had to use his or her ration cards at the market and it was tough going. Hotels and restaurants, however, weren't required to abide by rationing when they sold food, but the government had limited the prices and the menus and the war had pretty much taken care of the rest. The menus weren't what anyone who frequented five star hotels would expect, but the fare was still a far cry better than what the average citizen of London could manage to cobble together with ration points.

Their food ordered; Jack set about giving them a lesson in Spying 101.

"The first thing you've got to know are the players. Sometimes I think half of London is spying on the other half. See the two leaving now? The one tall one with the mustache and pinched face who looks like he's about to sneeze, he always looks like that by the way, with the pin-stripes? That's Jozef Karski: Polish, zero sense of humor, a heck of a lot stronger than he looks and too good with a knife. The other one, balding, with the sallow complexion and thick features is Yuri Lushinkov: Russian, expert marksman and a helluva dancer."

"Should you be telling us all this here? Out in the open?" Elizabeth asked.

"None of this is exactly top secret. Everyone knows who everyone else is. Most of us know what everyone else is doing. The devil's in the details. And speak of the devil," he said nodding his head toward a man sitting alone on the far side of the room. "Alex Stefanos. Greek and a crueler son of a bitch, I have never met. Keep your eye on him."

He *was* scary looking. His face was oddly asymmetrical; the effect was definitely discombobulating.

Jack checked his watch and grinned before looking up. "Right on cue."

Elizabeth followed his glance toward the entrance and a small, fastidious and well-dressed man. He caught sight of them and waved a gloved hand.

"Juris Zāle. Latvian," Jack explained. "Don't let him fool you, he's probably the most clever one of the bunch."

Elizabeth racked her brain trying to remember anything about Latvia. All she could manage was that it was one of the Baltics and was sandwiched between Russia and a couple other -ias.

Zāle held out his arms expansively in greeting. "Wells! My American friend, how are you?" He bowed at the waist. His accent was a Greek-Russian lovechild. "I don't mean to interrupt your luncheon, although I am quite put out that you have been keeping this one to yourself."

He stood staring at Elizabeth waiting for a proper introduction.

"Oh, sorry," Jack said. "Elizabeth, Juris. Juris, Elizabeth."

Zāle rolled his eyes. "Americans." He tugged off his glove and kissed Elizabeth's hand.

"That makes two of us," she said.

"Oh, my foot is in my mouth, is it not?" he said and pretended to spit it out. "How embarrassing. I make up for it with champagne."

He waived to a waiter across the room and made a circular gesture toward the table. "May I?" Before Jack could answer, he pulled out a chair and sat down. It was really more of a graceful sprawl. For such a small man, he took up an awful lot of room. He took off his other white glove and straightened his cravat.

Juris fixed Elizabeth with velvety, and absolutely outrageous, bedroom eyes. "You are enchanting. We must dine together. I have eggs in my room. I will peel them for you myself. And we will make love while the war rages outside our chambers."

Elizabeth half expected to see Simon lunge across the table or at the very least fire off some brilliant retort, but Simon merely sat there, leaning back in his chair, one long leg crossed over other, inscrutably calm. Jack smirked, enjoying the show.

"Juris," Wells said, "this is Simon Cross, Elizabeth's husband."

"Hoopsie, there goes the other one!" he said with a laugh. "Good thing I only have two feet, no?" He waved his gloves in apology. Abruptly, he stood and bowed. "Mr. Cross," he said in a serious and dignified tone before plopping back down in his chair. He leaned over to Jack, nodded toward Simon and whispered loudly, "Is he going to hit me?"

Simon casually fingered the stem of his water glass and regarded the little man with mild amusement.

"I don't think so," Jack said. "At least not yet."

The waiter arrived with a bottle of champagne and four glasses.

"In that case, we drink!" Juris said.

The waiter made a show of opening the bottle the bottle and pouring the glasses. Juris carefully slid his glass to the edge of the table and grasped it by the base. He raised it in a toast, "Prieka!"

He took a sip, rolled his eyes and squirmed in ecstasy.

Elizabeth tried not to giggle and sipped her wine. Champagne made her silly, sillier than usual, and always left her regretting it.

"Quite good actually," Simon said inspecting the bubbles.

Jack, who didn't look like he drank much champagne, downed the entire glass in one swig and fought back an oncoming burp.

"Philistine," Juris said, but then quickly added. "Do not mis-understand. I am glad the Americans are here, especially you," he said as he patted the back of Elizabeth's hand. "The soldiers are useful, but not such pleasant company."

"Thank you."

"So, our friend Jack is giving you the skimpy."

"The skinny," Jack corrected.

"Yes, skinny, this is what I mean. The key—may I?" he asked Jack.

"Sure."

"Everyone gets caught up in all of this," Juris said motioning around the room. "They try to outsmart each other and see who can throw a knife the farthest. But this is not how the game is really played. It is not out there. It is in here." He tapped her head and then pointed to her chest. "And here." His finger and gaze lingered a little too long. "Oh, to play a game there."

Elizabeth nearly laughed out loud.

"Now that's a come-on," Jack said with a grin.

"You wound me. A come-on? Pffft. I am trying to make love to a beautiful woman," he said quickly glancing at Simon, "but I should do it with no hands." He held up his hands to show Simon who looked a little less amused than before.

"I'd rather you didn't do it at all," Simon said.

"I seem to have discovered a third foot." He stood and took Elizabeth's hand. "I am afraid I must pull myself away from your side." He leaned in and stage whispered, "If he should die in the war, most tragically, I would…"

Something close to a growl came from Simon as he stood up. He towered over Juris who had to bend his neck back to look up at Simon. "You are very tall."

Elizabeth was about to scold Simon for going needlessly Cro-Magnon when she saw the smile tugging at his lips. "Mr. Zale," Simon said with a slight incline of his head.

Juris looked once more anxiously at Simon, bowed to them all in turn, flashing Elizabeth his best "I still want you" look and scurried away.

Jack laughed out loud.

"He's harmless," Elizabeth said.

Simon sat down, quite satisfied with himself. "Don't be so sure."

"Philistine," Jack said with a grin.

The rest of lunch was more of the same. Jack pointed out several more spies, including a man from Luxembourg, Paul Majerus, who was so stylish he actually pulled off wearing a cape, and an attractive French woman, Michele Renaud, who was cold and beautiful and a dead ringer for Coco Chanel.

After lunch, Jack brought them back to his suite. First thing he did was turn on his wireless set and find some American big band music. The first time Elizabeth didn't think anything of it. Now, she realized it was to interfere with any listening devices. The music would make it nearly impossible for any of the old equipment to pick up their conversation cleanly.

"So," Jack said. "What did you learn at the hospital?"

Elizabeth opened her mouth to speak, but Simon interrupted.

"Nothing yet," he said. "He recognized us, but he's not quite all there yet."

"He didn't say anything about the Shard?"

Elizabeth and Simon had discussed whether they should trust Jack and, not surprisingly, had disagreed. In the end, Simon's logic had won out. A gambler never shows his cards before he has to. But now, under Jack's probing stare, Elizabeth wasn't sure she could keep the truth from him.

Simon stepped into the void. "I think we can make progress with more visits though. It's going to take some time, I'm afraid."

Elizabeth felt the weight of Jack's eyes on her and tried to concentrate on the music. If she looked him in the eyes, he'd know she was lying. She was sure of it. Luckily, Jack didn't push the matter. If he didn't believe Simon, he gave no sign of it.

"Can't expect miracles, I guess."

"No," Simon said. "And in the meantime, I'd like to do a little research. I'm a little rusty on a few points."

"About the Shard?"

"And the mythos it comes from. You never know what sort of detail might be important."

"That makes sense," Jack said. "Where do you go to do something like that?"

"I doubt the library will have much, but it's certainly worth a try. I was thinking about exploring a few antiquarian bookshops. It might be a fool's errand, but there are a few volumes I'd very much like to see. Of course, there's *Nibelungenlied,* and *Aesir & Venir, The Codex Regius.* And I think it would be wise to refresh my memory of the *Oyenskitter Grimoire.* It's been years since I researched Wotan and Norse mythology. Oh, and perhaps even an original text of the *Volsungs.* That would be fascinating."

"Fascinating," Jack said, clearly not as excited as Simon.

She had to give Simon a lot of credit. He'd done a masterful job of giving them a legitimate reason to look for the book Evan had mentioned without drawing attention to it. She was going to have to get wily and fast if she was going to keep up and not give up the game.

"He gets that way with research," Elizabeth said. "I think it's kind of sexy."

It was clear Jack couldn't wrap his mind around that. "If you say so. I'll leave the professoring to you. Just be careful. Hans might be dead, but I doubt it. He's a tough son of a bitch."

She'd been so caught up in everything else, she'd managed to push that to the back of her mind. It was a sobering though. For a wake-up call, nothing beats having a Nazi killer after you.

"Do you think he'll come after us again?" she asked.

"Probably not."

"Probably?" Simon said. "Forgive me if I fail to find that reassuring."

"It isn't meant to be." Jack frowned and shook his head. "I wish you two weren't mixed up in this, but there's no way out now. If Hans knew you were the key to what Eldridge knows about the shard, then five'll get you ten, everybody else does too. And, don't kid yourself, this game is for keeps. If it gets them what they want, every one of those charming people downstairs will put a bullet in your skull without thinking twice."

The excitement from a few minutes ago fled in a hurry.

"The stakes are about as high as they can get," Jack continued. "I don't know if I believe all this mystical stuff, but if this shard thing can give them the edge, we sure as hell better get to it first."

Chapter Twelve

"Do you think we're being followed?" Elizabeth asked as they stood together in the crowded underground car.

"No doubt," Simon said, "but remember what Wells said. This Hans or anyone else isn't likely to try anything in broad daylight in front of witnesses."

"Right." She let go of her handhold and wrapped her arms around Simon's neck. "It is kind of exciting."

"The entire business is horrifying, ill-conceived and foolhardy," he said as he frowned deeply. "The only exciting thing will be if we manage to survive."

Elizabeth pouted. "The only thing?"

He let out a deep breath and pulled her closer. His frown melted away, mostly, and was replaced with something definitely smoldery. "No, not the only thing."

She grinned and pushed herself up on tiptoes to kiss him.

The next thing she knew people around her were shouldering to get out.

"This is us," Simon said. "Tottenham Court."

The surge of people exiting the station carried them up the stairs and they spilled out onto the corner of Tottenham Court Road and Charing Cross.

Simon took his bearings. "It's a pity the museum is closed."

"The British Museum?" She'd always wanted to go there. It was one of those magical places where the past met the present. It was a feeling she knew all too well.

"I'm afraid all of the collections are housed in underground facilities to protect them from bombing."

Simon must have read her mind or at the very least seen the disappointment in her face. "When we return home, we'll go. I think you'd enjoy it. But for now," he said, nodding down Charing Cross Road, "we have a book to find."

They'd agreed never to ask about just *The Book of Iona*, but always be sure to include several other volumes in each inquiry. Simon had given her a list of other tomes they could throw into the mix to keep everyone guessing. At least that was the plan.

They walked south down Charing Cross Road, which slowly led them back toward home. The first two stores were a complete bust, but the third seemed promising. The owner had at least heard of *The Book of Iona*. It was a late 15th century book of poetry with no real significance other than its age and scarcity. He suggested they try another seller just past Leicester Square. They bought two small, irrelevant books and left.

As Simon and Elizabeth left the shop, she noticed a couple window-shopping across the street. It was Renaud and Majerus, the French woman and the man from Luxembourg. Even though they weren't Russian, she thought of them as her own personal

Boris and Natasha. But really, if Majerus was trying to blend in, he should have traded his cape for a Chesterfield at the very least.

"We've got company," Elizabeth said rolling her eyes in the direction that they were standing.

Simon nodded. "Yes, I saw them. I think the Russian's behind us."

"Spies on parade!"

"Elizabeth," Simon chided as he choked back a laugh.

"How about one more shop then back to the hotel. I don't want to be wandering around after dark if we can help it." The afternoon sun was already beginning to dip behind the brick buildings that lined the street.

"Agreed."

John Smith's Bookshoppe smelled like dust and tea and stillness. A little old man, who must have been eleven hundred years old, peered at them over tiny spectacles as the bell rang announcing their entrance. Stacks of books teetered precariously in the aisles and stretched nearly from floor to ceiling. Shelves overflowed with books. Every nook and cranny had a volume tucked into it. They carefully inched their way between the bookcases.

Cookbooks were mixed in with medieval armor and Oscar Wilde with Alexander Pope. If there was a method to the madness, it was lost on them. After a few minutes of aimless wandering, Simon picked his way back to the front desk.

"Excuse me," Simon said. "I'm looking for a few particular volumes."

"A place for everything and everything in its place," the little man said with a slight Irish accent and even slighter interest.

"Yes, to be sure. It's just that I can't quite figure out the way the books are organized. Is there a key?"

The man looked up at Simon and tapped his head with a bony finger. "All in here."

"Of course. You don't happen to have the *Codex Regius* or *Aesir & Venir?*"

The man squinted. "Yes and no. Back wall, center case, third shelf, red binding. Ten pounds. And to the other? No."

Simon was suitably appalled and impressed. "Ten quid? That's outrageous."

The man just shrugged.

"Hmph. I don't suppose you have the *Book of Iona?*"

"Did. Don't anymore. Don't expect to see it again."

"You did have it though."

Elizabeth heard the excitement in Simon's voice and joined him at the counter.

"That's what I said."

"If you don't mind my asking, what happened to it?"

The shopkeeper frowned up at Simon and pursed his lips. "It sprouted legs and walked out. What do you think happened to it? It sold."

"Do you know who bought it?" Elizabeth asked.

"Of course, I do. I'm old, not daft."

"Whom did you sell it to?" Simon asked.

"Whom," the man said with displeasure, "I sell my books to is my business and not yours."

"Couldn't you make an exception?" Elizabeth asked. "Just this one time?"

The little man was about to say something sour when he noticed the two ten pound notes Simon had place on the counter.

"For the Codex," Simon said.

The shopkeeper nearly drooled at the sight of so much money. Twenty pounds was a month's pay for most men in 1942. His hands shook as he took it.

"Well, what are you waiting for, girl? Go get the book."

When Elizabeth returned with the book, he scribbled something onto a receipt pad and wrapped the book in crumpled brown paper. He handed them both to Simon.

"The name?"

The man waggled a finger at the receipt.

Simon turned it over and scrawled in barely legible script was a name and partial address. "Thank you."

The man nodded, pursed his lips and waved them to the door. "Now, get out."

Simon held the door open for Elizabeth and they both heard the door lock behind them. The hastily turned "closed" sign swung behind the glass. Simon put the receipt into his breast pocket and tucked their bundle under his arm.

"Bloomsbury isn't far," he said, "It's just back by the museum and the university. I think the address is a business or an office, and it's got to be near five by now. I think we'd better wait until tomorrow."

Elizabeth looked back at their shadows and hoped they'd wait too.

The streets were emptying as the sun set, but they were still awash with every uniform imaginable—Canadian, Free French, and American. Sometimes the Americans seemed to outnumber the Londoners. Always trailing along behind a band of US soldiers, the "snowdrop" or MP with his white helmet kept the men in line. Mostly.

Austerity took the fun out of most things a soldier on leave usually enjoyed—movies, nightclubs and late-night carousing. There were a few dance clubs and canteens, but entertainment was generally hard to come by.

Elizabeth saw a sign about a dance and was just about to ask Simon about it when the siren came. At first, the sound was off in the distance, but as other sirens closer to them began to wail, it was a loud and insistent two-tone warble.

"Air raid?" she asked. It was a stupid question, but she was giving herself a pass. It was her first war, her first air raid and, quite possibly, her first panic attack.

Simon's gentle grip on her elbow became a vise. "This way." His voice was as tight as her stomach.

She looked up, straining to see the bombers, but the sky was just a steely gray. The sirens and Simon insisted she stop dawdling and get a move on.

They fell in with the crowd since they seemed to know where they were going. An air raid warden with his trademark helmet blew his whistle and waved people toward the shelter that was also marked by large signs with arrows pointing the way.

No one ran, but they weren't casual about it either. They moved quickly, but there was no panic. The omnipresent "Keep Calm and Carry On" signs seemed to be doing their job. It was very much business as usual. And after three years of bombing, it was no wonder. Children giggled with delight and pretended to be manning the anti-aircraft guns or engaging in spitfire dogfights. Others dragged their feet and shuffled along in that wonderfully put-upon way only children can.

The moan of the sirens faded as they went further down into one of the Underground shelters. An elderly woman struggled down the stairs. Simon took one arm and Elizabeth took the other as they helped the woman down the final steps. All around them, people were doing the same thing. If someone needed help, it was given. Children who were separated from parents were looked after until they were found. No one shoved. Everyone made room as best they could as people continued to stream in until the platform was filled to bursting. Some people had blankets and appeared to have somehow beaten the sirens to the punch.

"It's not as common as it was during the Blitz," Simon explained as they found a spot along the wall to wait it out. "But before dark, some Londoners leave their homes and apartments in a nightly migration to the Underground shelters. They'll stay here every night."

The atmosphere was shockingly normal, even pleasant. It was almost as though they were having a campout or enjoying a night at the canteen and not huddled in a subway tunnel. A little white rabbit hopped through the crowd with a boy not much bigger in chase.

His mother brought up the rear of the little parade. "Charlie! I've told you it's not a pet to be carried about."

"Monty!" Charlie snatched up the rabbit, giving him a few quick soothing pets before stuffing Monty into his coat. He looked up defiantly at his mother. The little rabbit's head poked out of his coat and seemed to do the same. "It's bad luck to eat the white ones, mum. That's what Billy said."

"Billy's been telling you porkies."

"He wouldn't."

The mother sighed, took little Charlie by the hand and dragged him back through the crowd. "Billy!"

Poor bunny, and poor Charlie. She'd read that the government encouraged people not to just grow their own vegetables, but to raise rabbits, chickens and even pigs in their gardens, if they could. She'd even seen a few public allotments for pig clubs. It was a clever way to increase food production. Nearly every bit of available space including backyards, public parks and even window boxes were used to grow things or raise them. But when push came to butcher, she wasn't sure she'd have the stomach to do the deed. It was just something else she was grateful she didn't have to endure.

"Maybe Monty will be one of the lucky ones," Simon said.

Elizabeth leaned into Simon and rested her head against his chest. "I hope so."

CHAPTER THIRTEEN

AFTER LESS THAN HALF an hour the air raid warden told them it was over. Just like that, the tunnel emptied and life restarted. When the all-clear siren, a single-toned blast, stopped, the world became unnaturally quiet. Dusk had passed and the streets fell into that singular darkness brought by the blackout.

They caught one of the last big, red double-decker buses for the day and, despite the chill, rode on the top deck back to the hotel. A single chimney of smoke rose from a fire in the distance.

When they got back to their rooms Elizabeth felt the grime of the day caked on her skin. She shivered to think about what the city must have been like back in Dickens' day when the air was thick with coal smoke. A bath before dinner was definitely in order.

Clean and feeling refreshed, she wrapped one of the towels around herself and went into the bedroom to dress. Simon was lying down in the middle of the bed reading the book he'd bought earlier and looking damn hot doing it.

His shoes and socks were off, his long legs crossed at the ankles. His white shirtsleeves were rolled up to mid-forearm, one hand behind his head propping it up on the pillows as the other held the book. Only Simon could make reading in a sweater vest sexy.

He lowered the book and peered at her over the edge of the binding. She saw the smile in his eyes. He laid the book down on his chest and stared at her.

"What?" she said, checking to see if she had something stuck to her face.

"You are so beautiful."

No matter how often he said that it still made her blush.

"You're biased."

He closed the book, put it on the side table and rolled onto his side. "Infinitely." He got up and walked slowly toward her. "But that doesn't make it any less true."

He ran a finger over the still damp skin of her shoulder and along the hollow of her collarbone. With excruciating tenderness, his hand touched the side of her neck and then cupped her cheek. He leaned in as he urged her closer. The kiss was soft and gentle, but anything but chaste. There was a feeling of tethered restraint behind each touch. When Simon pulled away, his eyes were so dark with love and desire it made her tremble.

He swept her into his arms and carried her to the bed. The towel fell open as he laid her down on the comforter. One knee on the edge of the bed, he leaned down and kissed her neck with passion he'd been holding back.

Elizabeth's breath caught in her throat.

He grasped one wrist and held it down on the bed as he feverishly kissed her neck and jaw.

A horrible realization interrupted Elizabeth's otherwise very pleasant thoughts. "Do you think they're watching us?" she asked breathlessly. "Right now?"

Simon barely paused long enough to answer her. "Who?"

"The spy people."

"Let them," he said as he pulled off his vest and they both worked on the buttons of his shirt. "Maybe they'll learn something."

His shirt partially undone, he dove back down for another searing kiss and Elizabeth stopped caring about anything else.

The next day, they took the Tube up to Bloomsbury to Professor Giles' office where the bookseller had directed them yesterday. It was in one of the many buildings that made up the many colleges that made up the University of London. Luckily, Giles was more than happy to accommodate a visiting professor. He was the quintessential absent-minded type—tall, tortoise shell glasses, a bit of a potbelly and wisps of hair that curled away from his head like dozens of unruly thoughts escaping. The gleam in his eyes when Simon asked about the various codices meant she'd be sure to lose them both in details well beyond her scope of knowledge.

They'd found a ridiculously large book on the professor's dusty top shelf that had a color plate depicting the sword Nothung. They discussed the intricacies of Norse mythology while she did her best to recreate the image on a piece of paper. She sketched several other items to belie the importance of the sword.

Her art skills left a lot to be desired, but she managed a fair rendering. The sword in the plate was enormous, nearly four feet long with an extremely tapered point. The pommel was in the shape of an eagle, wings extended. The grip was covered with interwoven snakes and the guard looked something like horns. The blade itself was typical of most great swords, except for two things—the jagged edge that ran a full two feet down the edges of the top half of the blade beneath the hilt and the runes that were etched on its surface.

Elizabeth did her best to copy everything as precisely as possible. Several of the runes were frighteningly familiar. "Is this what I think it is?" she asked pointing to the jagged S-shaped rune.

Simon and the professor leaned over her shoulder.

"Oh, yes, the Sig rune," the professor said. "It was originally a rune for the sun called Sowoli. But of course, the Nazis corrupted it as they did with so many other things. Here." He pointed to more runes. "This one and this one here used to have entirely different meanings. Now, they're symbols of the virtues of SS officers. Faith in the cause and self-sacrifice."

The professor's gaze lingered on the sword. "That is an unusual piece, isn't it? I'm not sure I've ever quite seen that particular configuration of runes before."

They'd done their best to disguise their interest in the sword with more general questions about mythology. The last thing they needed was for the professor to fixate.

"They've done that a lot, haven't they?" Elizabeth asked. "Take pagan symbols and turn them into something else?"

"Yes!" the professor said happy to expound on the subject. "They're quite adept actually at usurping other religions and turning them to their own purposes. Both from Christianity and Paganism. You'll see symbols and even rituals that might once have been a celebration of the winter solstice warped into parts of an SS dinner party."

"Sounds more like a religion than a political party."

"Yes, doesn't it?" the professor said as he scanned his bookshelves. "I've often thought as much myself. Himmler in particular is rather adept at using mythology and the occult to increase the zeal of his men, or so I hear. Not that I hear much. The hallowed walls of academia can be terribly thick sometimes."

"I know the feeling," Simon said.

"Supposedly," Giles said, "Himmler and Hitler admire the epic struggles often found in Norse mythology and even in stories of the Holy Grail. Parsifal in particular."

"That's another Wagner opera, isn't it?" Elizabeth hadn't forgotten everything Simon had tried to teach her about opera.

"Yes, they both share a great affinity for his work," Giles said. "Personally, I've always found it rather overwrought."

"Agreed." Simon said. "You've been so very helpful with our research, I'm hesitant to ask too much of you, but I was wondering about something else. We were at Smith's bookshop and he mentioned that you'd bought a copy of *The Book of Iona*. I don't suppose you have it here. I've been searching for it. For a colleague."

"Smiths…" Giles took off his glasses and chewed thoughtfully on the earpiece. "*The Book of Iona*…oh, yes!"

Elizabeth and Simon exchanged quick, excited glances. This was the moment they'd been waiting for.

"But I'm afraid I don't have it here."

So much for the moment.

"I don't actually have it at all anymore. It's funny you should say you wanted it for a colleague. I bought it for a dear friend. Was his birthday present as a matter of fact. Sometime last month. I can't remember precisely."

"Pity," Simon said looking at Elizabeth for help.

"Is he a professor too?" Elizabeth asked.

"Yes, although he doesn't teach anymore. He's a bit of an odd duck, you see. Regardless, I have to say he is the most talented linguist I've ever known. Rupert Morley. Has a place over in Cirencester."

They thanked Professor Giles for his time and it was all Elizabeth could do not to run out of his office and all the way to

Cirencester. That was until Simon told her it was about a hundred miles away. Both her feet and her stomach protested against the idea of running that far. They agreed to have lunch first and then save the world.

They found a large cafeteria. Simon explained that it was one of the hundreds of British Restaurants the government controlled in an attempt to keep food costs down and its citizens fed. They had Welsh Rarebit, which Elizabeth always thought had actual rabbit in it (Run, Monty, run!), but ended up being just burnt toast and a tangy cheese sauce. The side dish was, ironically, carrots. They split a piece of victory sponge for dessert. An actual sponge might have been better. But, Elizabeth was determined to eat every mouthful. She had a bad case of the guilts.

"You don't have to finish it," Simon said.

"I do." She forced down the last bit. "Everything I don't eat is something someone more needy needs. Needier needs? Either way, it's less for someone else."

"I don't think one bite of cake is going to make a difference."

"Maybe not, but—" The rest of her sentence died in her throat.

"What's wrong?" Simon asked.

The hair on the back of Elizabeth's neck stood on end as a cold chill ran through her. Sitting at a table less than twenty feet away was the German, Hans. She took a calming breath and didn't answer the panic knocking at the door.

Simon followed her gaze. "Dammit. Come on," he said as he urged her to get up. She sure as heck didn't need urging.

They tried to move casually, but every sound, every movement felt like a claxon going off announcing, "We're here!" They hurried to the door and slipped outside. They'd barely gone twenty feet when Elizabeth looked behind her. The door to the restaurant flew open and Hans spilled out onto the sidewalk. His face was pale, making the red from his scar look angrier than before. He scanned the crowd and found them easily. He sneered and set out after them.

"Not good," she said. "He saw us."

"This way." Simon pulled her across the street.

Once they were on the other side, they wove their way through the pedestrian traffic. It was mid-afternoon and the streets were filled with people, most of whom it seemed were going in the opposite direction. Elizabeth desperately searched for a policeman or even an air raid warden. Someone. Where was a marauding band of GIs when you really needed them?

As they hurried through the crowd, she saw a big blue police box and a ridiculous series of thoughts tumbled one after the other through her mind. Maybe Dr. Who was there? She idly wondered which doctor it would be. No, it was a real police box and not a Tardis. Darn it. But, police were good. They could go inside and call for the police. That's what the boxes were for, after all. They could go inside and be trapped like rats while they waited for an unarmed police officer to come from some station a block or more away and defeat the patient Nazi who would surely wait and not just kill them.

They ran past the police box and Simon pulled Elizabeth toward a Tube entrance, which was really little more than a sandbag bunker above a hole in the ground. Elizabeth nearly slipped as they hurried down a short set of steps and through the main concourse. They ran past the ticket booth and down an absurdly enormous escalator before Simon yanked her into an offshoot tunnel. After another long, narrow corridor, they headed down an even longer set of stairs. At the bottom, they ran through an archway and onto a crowded platform.

Simon's grip on her hand was so tight it hurt, but she sure as heck wasn't about to complain or let go. They serpentined through the crowd toward the far end of the tunnel. A train pulled into the station and brought a blast of warm air with it. Elizabeth looked back and saw Hans weaving his way through the crowd. One hand was stuffed into his jacket pocket and she knew he was holding a gun.

The train doors opened and a wave of people washed out. She lost sight of Hans for a moment as he struggled against the tide. But he reappeared a second later and their eyes met. The coldness in his expression took her breath away.

"He's right behind us."

Simon yanked on her hand again and they tried to duck out through one of the exits, but it was so packed with people, they couldn't get through and had to press on down the tunnel. The further they went the thinner the crowd became. Finally, they reached the end, an aptly named dead end.

They turned back just in time to see a man stumble into Hans. It looked like they were arguing, but it was difficult to tell because Elizabeth couldn't see the other man's face. Hans tried to shove the man away, but he held on to Hans' arms.

The interruption gave them what they needed, a chance to run for the exit. They started for the archway.

Hans suddenly fell back against the tiled wall, his shoulders hunched and a hand clutching his stomach. The other man stepped back and helped Hans slide down the wall as though he were instantly drunk. Hans slid all the way down until his chin was resting on his knees. The other man patted his shoulder in a friendly manner. The man straightened Hans' hat before he stood back up and then turned to face Elizabeth and Simon.

The last thing she expected was to recognize his face. And when she did, her heart flipped. It was Evan's doctor from Guy's hospital.

"Dr. Webber?"

Dr. Webber wiped the blade of his knife on Han's coat, folded it and slipped it into his coat pocket. His expression was flat and unreadable.

Elizabeth looked up at Simon. He'd seen it too. He jerked on her hand and pulled her back toward the crowd. "Come on."

They ran for the exit and melted in with the crowd as it poured through the corridor, up the wooden-planked escalator, more stairs, past the ticket collector who shouted something after them and finally outside. Elizabeth didn't know what to think. What on earth was Evan's doctor doing there and why had he just killed Hans? She supposed she should be grateful for that last part, but not knowing why he was there and who he really was scared the bejesus out of her.

Everything was all harumscarum now. Her heart pounded as she caught her breath. "What just happened?"

Simon didn't have an answer.

"Evan," she said, gripping his hand. "We've got to get to the hospital." What if the doctor had already done something to him and they were too late? But then why would he hurt Evan? Why was he following them? He'd killed Hans, which was a good thing, she tried to tell herself, but the idea made her sick anyway. He'd just murdered a man. What had seemed straightforward before was suddenly a twisted Mobius strip.

Simon flagged down a taxi and they both silently urged it to go faster as it headed toward the Thames and Guy's hospital on the other side. Simon paid the cabbie and they hurried toward the wing where Evan was. All they found at the end of their journey was another dead end. They were politely informed that Evan was not allowed to see visitors—doctor's orders. It wasn't hard to guess what doctor. Elizabeth wasn't sure what she'd expected. It was naïve to think they could just walk out with Evan after everything that had happened.

What if Evan wasn't even at the hospital anymore? What if he'd been moved? They'd come here to save him and now he was probably God only knew where. Stymied at the hospital, they went back to the hotel. Maybe Jack could help them. He'd know what was going on.

Simon knocked loudly on Jack's door. "Wells!"

"All right, all right," came Jack's voice from inside the room. "Keep your shirt on." He opened the door and stood aside for them to enter. Harry James' Sleepy Lagoon played softly in the background.

"We just saw Hans," Elizabeth said breathlessly. "He chased us and we ran. But then the doctor, Evan's doctor, he was there and, I think he stabbed Hans."

"I know," Jack said.

"We were—" Simon started. "What do you mean, you know?"

The bathroom door opened and Dr. Webber stepped out, casually drying his hands with a towel. "I told him."

Chapter Fourteen

Dr. Webber tossed the towel back into the bathroom. "I'm sure you have questions," he said as he rolled down his shirtsleeves and re-buttoned the cuffs.

Elizabeth arched an eyebrow. "Just a few."

Simon edged in front of her. "Stay where you are."

"Relax," Jack said. "He's one of the good guys."

"I like to think so." The doctor grabbed his jacket from the back of the chair. "Andrew Blake, British Intelligence."

Another spy? She needed a scorecard. "Is anyone in London who they seem to be?"

"You might be the only ones," Blake said with a smile.

If only he knew.

Blake stepped forward and offered Simon his hand. "I apologize for the ruse, but I assure you, it was necessary."

Reluctant at first, Simon eventually shook it. "You're not a doctor then?"

"Heavens, no. Can't stand the sight of blood."

"You didn't seem to mind it a few hours ago," Elizabeth said. The memory of Hans' stabbing and Blake's cold face were at odds with the easy-going charm of the man in front of her.

"Nasty business," he said. "Please?" He gestured for them to sit.

Elizabeth sat in the corner of the sofa, but Simon remained standing behind her. Blake took a chair opposite hers and offered her a cigarette from a silver case in his pocket. When she declined, he tapped the end of his cigarette against the case and then lit it with a matching silver lighter.

"Why were you following us?" Elizabeth asked.

Blake plucked a stray fragment of tobacco from the tip of his tongue. "I wasn't following you. I was following Hans, whose real name, by the way, is Heinrich Bernhardt, SS. We've been watching him and his partner for several months now." He took a deep drag from his cigarette.

"Apparently," he continued, slowly exhaling the smoke, "they were involved in the killing of the two Swedish agents near Swindon. It's possible they were responsible for the injuries Eldridge suffered. He was in bad shape when we found him."

"You found Evan?" Elizabeth asked.

"We took him to the infirmary, did our best to help him regain his health and hoped he could help us recover the Shard. But, it hasn't quite worked out that way."

"His memory," Elizabeth said.

"Is selective," Blake said. "We are quite aware that he is not as ill as he appears."

That definitely wasn't what Elizabeth wanted to hear. She really thought they had that one advantage over everyone else and now even that was gone. It made her wonder what else they knew and weren't saying.

"Eldridge has kept his own counsel," Blake continued. "Until now."

"You two weren't the first people to visit him at Guy's hospital," Jack said. "But you were the only ones he spoke to."

"That makes you rather special," Blake said.

Elizabeth turned to look up at Simon and they shared an uneasy glance.

"We're family," Elizabeth said quickly. Perhaps too quickly.

Blake smiled enigmatically, but if he knew they were lying he didn't press the point. "Yes and word of your relationship and visit has spread."

Simon stepped forward so that he was at Elizabeth's side. "There's still something I don't understand."

Elizabeth's brain was having trouble keeping up. "Just one thing?"

Jack chuckled.

"How did the Germans know about our flat that first night?" Simon asked. "We'd only just arrived. No one knew where we were staying except for staff at Guy's."

"Including myself," Blake added for him. "Yes, I'm afraid we have a bit of a mole problem. Several of the staff are MI5 and it seems one of them is a double-agent. Your whereabouts weren't the first piece of leaked information we've discovered." The ash on his cigarette had grown precariously long and Jack slid the ashtray toward him. He tapped the end off and continued. "That's one of the reasons I was following Bernhardt this afternoon. I'd received word that he might be meeting with our mole. I trailed him into the restaurant where, well, you know the rest of that story."

"I suppose we owe you our thanks," Simon said. "For saving our lives."

Blake demurred the compliment with a shake of his head. "I'm sorry you had to see it," he said to Elizabeth. "I'm sure that was quite upsetting."

Elizabeth's emotions on the subject weren't just mixed they were pureed. "I know he was the enemy and probably would have done worse to us if you hadn't, but killing…I don't know if I'll ever get used to it."

"Nor should you," Blake said. "Taking another man's life should never be done lightly."

"Got to admit, I'm not gonna lose any sleep over a Kraut like Hans," Jack said. "Sick SS bastards. Pardon my French."

"Well, be that as it may," Blake said. "We have a more pressing problem. Eldridge is being moved. Whether Mother is tired of the lapses in security or it's somehow the work of the mole, our time is running out."

Jack was suddenly all business. "Where are they taking him?"

"The Cage."

"That's not good," Jack said.

"What's the Cage?" Simon asked.

"An…interrogation facility," Blake said clearly meaning more than that. "Once he's there, M19 takes over and I can't help him or you."

M19? How many Ms were there? "When is he being moved?"

"Tomorrow night. And," Blake continued, "I'm afraid he might not make it to his destination. He'll be terribly vulnerable en route."

"Right," Jack said. "And if you know, the mole knows. Whoever they work for, they can't afford for their only lead to the Shard to end up locked away in the hands of the War Office."

"Exactly."

"What can we do?" Elizabeth asked. They'd come all this way to save Evan. There had to be something they could do.

There was a long, silent pause as the men exchanged glances and Simon said what they were all thinking. "We get to him first."

Elizabeth smoothed the adhesive strip of the Band-Aid down against her heel and tossed the wrapper into the bathroom trashcan. The blister from her shoe was raw and irritated. A bit like Simon.

"It was your idea," she said as she secured the strap of her shoe, grabbed her eye pencil and went back into the bedroom.

Simon glared at her from the edge of the bed as he tied his shoe. "I don't like it."

"So you said." Elizabeth leaned against the doorway. "All last night and all through breakfast, again at lunch—"

"Please don't joke about it."

"I'm sorry," she said as she plopped down next to him. "I guess I'm a little nervous."

"We don't have to do this." He turned to her with his Very Serious face on. "In fact, I don't think we should."

"You don't mean that."

Simon started to argue, but only a sigh came out. "No."

"And that's why I love you."

"But I still don't like it."

Elizabeth stood back up. "It's a good plan."

"It's dangerous, reckless, and sure to end with imprisonment or worse."

"All the best plans do." She held out the eye pencil. "Would you?"

"Is that really necessary?"

"If I'm going to end up in some prison somewhere, I want to look my best, don't I?"

Simon shook his head in resignation and took the eye pencil. He motioned for her to turn around.

It was an odd thing to do, but stockings were in short supply and so, like every other fashion-conscious woman of the day, she drew on the stocking seam with a brown eye pencil. However, she never could get it straight.

"Lift up your skirt," Simon said.

"Why Mr. Cross!"

He twirled the pencil in the air. "Do you want your seams or not?"

Spoilsport. Just to irk him she lifted her skirt high and arched her back with a sigh. "I do."

"If you're trying to distract me," Simon said. "It's working."

She wiggled her bottom.

"But, if you want these straight," he said. "You'd better hold still."

She did and it was her turn to be distracted. Simon's hands were warm against her skin and she was sure he moved them in just that sensual way to drive her crazy. Somehow, he managed to draw the lines and then added a very small x at the top of her thigh.

"What's that for?"

"Just marking where I left off." He stood and turned her around to face him.

"In case you forget?" she said.

"Not possible." He kissed her and then tossed the pencil on the bed. "Ready?"

"As I'll ever be." She handed him his fedora and they left the safety of their room.

They rode down in the elevator in anxious silence. The city was as still and as dark as midnight. They stood in the shadows on the street in front of the hotel. Both of them wanted to speak, but neither could quite find the words. Finally, Elizabeth broke the uneasy silence.

"It's cold. Keep your hat on." She pulled the brim of his fedora down a bit more snuggly and needlessly straightened the lapel of his coat.

She could see Simon's jaw muscle working overtime.

"You don't need to say it," she said. "But the truth is I'm scared out of my gourd and it wouldn't hurt to hear a little reassurance."

Simon laughed lightly. "Do you really want me to placate you with false assurances?"

"Couldn't hurt."

"Everything is going to be all right," he said and then grew serious and caressed her cheek. "And you are the bravest person I've ever met."

"You need to get out more."

"Elizabeth…" He sighed again. "Promise me you'll be careful."

She nodded. It was her turn to not trust her voice.

"Good," he said. "I'll see you in a few hours."

Their kiss was sad and longing and over far too soon. Without another word spoken, they turned away from one another and walked off alone into the cold English night.

CHAPTER FIFTEEN

ELIZABETH FELT LIKE A spy. Not that she had any idea what a spy really felt like, but she was pretty sure they felt like she did—a cross between elated and nauseous. She took the short tube ride from Westminster to Charing Cross where she transferred to the Northern Line up to Warren. She was inordinately pleased she'd managed to buy the right tickets and transfer to the right train. If only the rest of the night were so simple.

From there she walked to the Euston Square station where one of London's endless supply of big black taxis was waiting for her. Simon was on a similar circuitous journey in the other direction. All of the walking and transfers seemed silly at first, but they needed to do their best to trim their tails. No doubt, Boris and Natasha and several of the others would try to follow them. Along the way, she never did see anyone she recognized, but they were, unlike her, professionals. Maybe they were even using disguises. Maybe they were right next to her right now. She reined in her galloping paranoia and tried to focus. She had to trust that, with enough changes and double-backs, her trail was too difficult to follow and they'd be free to start the next stage of the operation - rescuing Evan.

Elizabeth slid into the back of the taxi and tried to calm down. She wanted adventure and, boy howdy, was she was getting it now. The mince pie she'd eaten earlier sloshed around threateningly in her stomach as the driver circled one of London's roundabouts several times. The whole thing was horrifying, but she had to admit, it was exciting too. Although, it all would have been a lot more exciting if Simon were with her. That part of the plan had been such a serious sticking point she thought Simon would never get unstuck. Both Jack and Blake insisted that she stay with them while Simon took Evan to a safe location. She couldn't really blame them. In many ways, they were actually sticking their necks out even further than she and Simon were. They certainly didn't want Simon and her to disappear into the night with Evan. If she stayed with them, Simon was sure to come back and the plan got bonus points for helping to confuse any other parties if they managed to keep up.

Simon only agreed to that part of the plan once they'd agreed to his stipulation that he choose the safe house for Evan and that location remained his secret. It was the only way to ensure the mole knew nothing of Evan's whereabouts.

In the end, and after enough blustering and arguing to put Congress to shame, they all agreed. Both stipulations meant each party entrusted the other with something critical. Trust wasn't easy to come by for Simon or Elizabeth these days, but she had no reason not to trust these men. Not one, but both of them had saved her life already. Jack had done it twice if she counted Zog. In her book, that was about as surefire a way to earn trust as there was. Simon wasn't so easily persuaded, but in the end, he gave in. Separating was the only way the plan would work. And if they wanted to keep Evan alive, they needed the plan to work.

Elizabeth's cab pulled up in front of a nondescript brick building somewhere in the northern part of London. She paid the fare and got out of the taxi. The noise of the car engine disappeared into the night. The street was quiet and nearly deserted. With no lights, and a thick even cloud cover, she could barely read the street numbers. She found number six and knocked three times in quick succession and then twice more slowly. She was disappointed that there wasn't a code word. Secret knocks really needed code words to round them out.

Jack opened the door and hurriedly ushered her inside. "Any problems?"

"No."

"Good." Jack led her down a dark hall to another door. Inside was a small working garage with two cars in it. One was up on blocks and the other pointed toward the door, ready to go. He checked his watch. "We've got a few minutes. You want something to drink? I think I still have a bottle of Coke I've been saving for a special occasion."

"Sure, thanks." Elizabeth had never considered herself a sugar addict until she was forced to go without it. It was in such short supply during the war that soft drink companies had all but stopped production. No sugar or soft drinks—it would be a great way to bring modern America to a screeching halt.

Jack came back with a bottle. "Found it."

The bottle was exactly the same as she remembered. It was nice to see that some things didn't change. He scanned around for glasses and found two cups. He rubbed one cleanish with a greasy rag and handed it to Elizabeth. There wasn't a bottle opener handy, so he used the edge of a tool cart to pop it open. He poured her cup half full. "It's warm."

"S'okay." Elizabeth took a sip and closed her eyes in pleasure. It was deliciously sweet. "Heaven."

"A little taste of home. Here." He wiped off a chair and pulled up a partner to it and sat down.

"Do you miss it?" she asked.

"The States? Some things, yeah." He thought about it for a moment and added, "Okay, a lot of things. You like baseball?"

"Dodger fan."

"Brooklyn? Sox," he said, tapping his chest. "Too bad they stink on ice. Your boys have a chance at the pennant. Who's your favorite?"

Oh, she was afraid he was going to ask that. She knew a little about baseball history. Her father had been a serious baseball nut. She tried to pull a name from a shelf in the back of her memory. "Pee Wee..."

"Reese? Good player."

Relief coursed through her. She'd been about to say Herman.

Jack stretched out his legs. "You know, I was pretty good. Played some high school ball. Could have gone pro, but..." he shook his head. She could tell it still stung after all these years. "Couldn't hit the curve." He mimicked a pitcher's windup. "It starts off here looking like one thing and then when it gets to you, it's something else."

"So you became a spy where everything is exactly as it appears."

Jack laughed. It was a comforting sound. "Yeah. Not right away though. You know how it is. Came from a nice middle class family, then the crash, and we had no class at all."

Elizabeth took another sip of Coke. It was wonderful and soothing her jumpy stomach. "What did you do?"

"Same as everybody else. Looked for work. I was on the south side of twenty. Did all sorts of things. Headed out West, even spent a few months in Ragtown down in Nevada. I'll tell ya, that was hard work."

Hard work in Nevada after the stock market crash meant one thing. "The dam."

"Moved a lot of rocks. Figured there had to be something better so I kept going west. Ended up in Hollywood. You ever see Texas Wind? Third Caballero," he said pointing his thumb at his chest in mock pride. "Also, The Lawless Rider Rides Again, I was Man Shot in Bank. Uncredited."

"Really? You were an actor?" He was handsome enough, but he didn't seem the type.

"Not really. I did stunts mostly. Faked my way through until I met Canutt and he showed me everything I was doing wrong." He turned his head to the side. "See this?"

There was a one-inch scar at the base of his skull just behind his ear.

"Ow."

"Jumped eight feet from a moving horse onto a wagon. Problem was the wagon was ten feet away.

Elizabeth lifted the hem of her skirt to show him a faded scar on the corner of her knee. "Bicycle. Curb. No training wheels."

"Impressive," he said. He pulled up his pant leg, pushed down his sock and showed her a long thin scar above his ankle. "Hit by a fire engine."

Elizabeth narrowed her eyes. "You were not."

"Was too. Only about so big though." He held his hands about six inches apart. "Was a toy. My brother's. But it still hurt." He nodded toward the top of her head. "How'd you get that one?"

Elizabeth's hand traced the small, crescent-shaped scar at the edge of her hairline on her forehead. "Exploding boat. Not a toy."

"You are going to have to tell me the rest of that story." He stood and checked his watch. "But it'll have to wait. You ready for this?"

"Not really."

"You'll be great. Just stick with the plan," Jack said. He added with a grin, "And when it's over, the first beer's on you."

Elizabeth and Jack had driven into position and all they had to do now was wait for the ambulance carrying Evan to drive past. Jack handed her a cardboard box. "Better put this on."

She opened the box. A gas mask. "We're not going to gas them, are we?"

"No, it'll cover our faces and distort our voices. Hurry up, put it on."

Elizabeth pulled the mask over her face. The eyeholes were huge and round, but set too far to the side. The entire contraption was hot and uncomfortable and had a horrible rubber smell. Worse yet, it was more than vaguely disturbing. She turned to Jack who looked like an alien from a fifties low-budget horror movie or bug-eyed elephant who'd lost his trunk.

The mask slid down her face until her nose was firmly planted between the eyeholes. Jack laughed and reached over to help her adjust the straps.

"Okay?" His voice was muffled through the filter.

She nodded that she was, but inside she definitely wasn't.

A few minutes later, the ambulance drove past right on schedule and Jack started the car and headed after it. No turning back now. After a few blocks, he floored the big sedan and they passed the ambulance. With a jerk of the big wheel, he swerved in front of them, cutting them off. Both vehicles came to a screeching halt. "Wait here until I give you the signal," Jack said as he jumped out of the car, guns in both hands.

"Don't move!" Jack yelled. "Hands. Let me see 'em. Don't move. Don't you dare move. Guns. I know you have 'em. Toss 'em. Slowly."

Elizabeth's breathing sped up so much she started to fog her goggles. Inside the confines of her mask, her heart was pounding so loudly and echoing in her ears, she almost missed Jack's signal.

She opened the door and came to the driver's side of the ambulance. The driver and the other man stayed in the cab and kept their hands in the air, their eyes fixed on the guns in Jack's hands.

"Give her the keys to the back," Jack said. "Slowly."

The driver did as he was instructed and tossed her a set of keys. She caught them and hurried to the back. She glanced around nervously. Where were Simon and Blake? She unlocked the door and sitting on the wooden planked side panel was Evan. He didn't move.

"We're here to rescue you," Elizabeth said in a loud whisper, feeling equal parts excited and idiotic.

Evan still didn't move. She realized what was wrong and lifted her gas mask up to show him her face. "It's me. Come on."

He seemed a little dazed, but clearly recognized her and started to crawl out of the van. Elizabeth heard footsteps behind her and whirled around. Dark silhouettes emerged from the blackness of the empty street. Her heart jumped rope - double-dutch—until she recognized one of the shadows. It was Simon, thank God, and next to him, Blake. They were careful to stay directly behind the ambulance and out of the line of sight of the side mirrors.

"Elizabeth?" Simon whispered.

She pulled up her gas mask again. "Shh. I'm fine. Take him."

Simon looked worried and frowned, but followed the plan. He gave Evan a hand out of the back of the ambulance, slipped off Evan's overcoat and handed it to Blake. With one last anxious look, Simon and Evan disappeared in the same direction they'd come, back down the street into the darkness, unseen, hopefully, by the driver and other attendant.

Blake shrugged on Evan's coat and Elizabeth wrapped a heavy woolen blanket over his shoulders, pulling it up just enough to obscure his face. He was the right height and build and if all went well, he'd be a dead ringer for Evan, hopefully without the dead part.

Blake hunched over and indicated that he was ready. Elizabeth took his elbow and led him back to the car in front of the ambulance. She kept herself between Blake and the driver, trying to shield him as best she could. It was only twenty feet, but it felt like a thousand. She opened the back door and Blake got in and slid across the seat. She followed him into the car and shut the door behind her, tossing the ambulance keys onto the floor of the car. Her heart was pounding again and the mask felt like it was closing in on her.

A moment later Jack jumped into the driver's seat, put the car in gear and roared off into the night. He took off his mask, tossed it onto the empty passenger seat and took a quick look back. "Smooth as silk."

"Well done," Blake said as he shucked his blanket covering. "You can take that off now, if you'd like."

Elizabeth pulled off her gasmask and took a deep breath of cold night air. "What now?"

"We head to the rendezvous point and hope everything goes well on their end," Jack said.

"And if it doesn't?" Elizabeth asked.

The car sped down a deserted street. Neither man had an answer for her.

CHAPTER SIXTEEN

SIMON COULD BARELY SEE the road in front of him. The car's shuttered headlights cast a pool of light that spread out perhaps all of ten feet in front of the car. Even at slow speeds it was dangerous going. It didn't help matters that the better part of his mind and all of his heart was fading behind him. He'd hated this part of the plan when they'd discussed it and he loathed it further still now that he and Elizabeth weren't just separated, but headed in opposite directions.

"You really shouldn't have come for me," Eldridge said in a voice dry and rough from disuse. "It's the Shard that's important."

"We haven't forgotten it, but it's currently beyond our grasp and," Simon said as he cast a glance at Eldridge, "as luck would have it, you were not."

"It's moved?"

"At least once. The book was sold and given as a gift to a man in Cirencester." Simon eased off the gas. As much as he wanted to deliver Evan to the safe house quickly, driving without headlights meant he'd have to slow down if he wanted to get there in one piece. "Elizabeth and I were going to look for it when news came of your impending transfer. We couldn't leave without at least trying to help you."

"I am grateful." Eldridge looked out into the dark of Greater London. He shifted in his seat uncomfortably. "I'm almost afraid to ask. I know the nature of time travel and leaving people behind. But, did you really see my wife?"

Simon could hear the fear and hope in his voice. "Yes."

"Is she all right? Was she?"

"She was fine." That was a bit of an overstatement. The last time he'd seen Lillian Eldridge she'd just survived the Great Quake and was facing raging fires, but technically, she was all right when they left.

"Thank God. When did you see her?"

Simon cast an anxious glance at Eldridge. He could only imagine how he'd react if he were in his place. "1906."

Eldridge nodded thoughtfully, processing the meaning of that year. "I see. And the house? It survived?"

"The quake? Yes, and I'm sure Gerald will take good care of your wife until we can return you to your home."

"Gerald is a good man," Eldridge said and drifted once more into silence. It was ten minutes at least until he spoke again. "It's strange; I've dreamt of going home every day since I've been here," he said, tugging nervously on his hands. "I didn't realize until just now that I never truly believed it would happen."

Simon smiled. "It will. If Elizabeth has anything to say about it."

"Your wife?"

Simon's hands tightened on the steering wheel. "Yes." He turned the car onto the A21.

Eldridge noticed the change of direction. "Where are we going?"

Simon leaned forward to peer into the darkness. With no signs and no lights, navigating the outskirts of London as they traveled into the agricultural green belt was tricky business. "Until we can sort out this business with the Shard, it's best if you're somewhere safe and secluded. There's a cottage in Hastings that's available and no one will bother you there."

"Surely, there's something I can do to help."

"There is. You'll tell me everything you know about the Shard."

Eldridge rubbed his temple. "I'll do my best, but not all of that back there in the hospital was an act. I can't even remember when I left Lillian. It could have been years ago or months. I can see her face, but I can't place the moment. It's an image with no context. I have a lot of those."

Eldridge paused in thought for a moment. "I remember things from my past. The further back the clearer they seem to be."

"Do you remember what your mission was?" Simon asked. He didn't want to push the man too hard, but they desperately needed information and he wasn't sure how long Eldridge could remain lucid and actively in the moment. "Why you came here? What you were supposed to do?"

"Find the Shard, confirm its existence and report back to the Council. Didn't they tell you that when they sent you?"

Simon hesitated before answering. "The Council didn't exactly send us. We're…freelancing."

Eldridge laughed. "They must be having fits."

The idea of the Council being in an uproar because of him gave Simon some pleasure. It was the least the bastards deserved. "My grandfather was a member. I am not." He briefly recounted his and Elizabeth's history with the watch, including how they'd accidentally activated it.

"That must have been a shocker." Eldridge's expression grew concerned. "What about my watch? Do you know where my watch is?"

"I was hoping you did."

Simon knew the loss of Eldridge's watch was a distinct possibility. Part of him had expected it really. After all, he was, by nature, a cautious, and some might even say pessimistic man, but surely even Schaupenhauer saw the glass as half full now and then.

"I hate to think of it out there in God knows whose hands," Eldridge said.

"We can only hope it's in a lockbox at MI5 headquarters and they're none the wiser as to what it does."

"I suppose." Eldridge sounded far from pleased at the notion. "But. "

"I have this ridiculous feeling I gave it to Winston Churchill."

Despite himself and despite the old man's fragile mental state, Simon couldn't help but smile at the thought.

"I know it's impossible," Eldridge continued. "Just an hallucination, I guess. Head trauma and pneumonia certainly do lead to interesting dreams. It's maddening though not knowing what's real and what's a figment of my own imagination. For all I know, you're not really here."

Simon hit a deep pothole in the road and they both bounced in their seats.

"Although," Eldridge said, "that felt pretty real."

The road grew even rougher, and enormous shell craters made it painfully slow going in some places. The car crept along on the dark road, winding its way through a maze of holes.

"If you weren't sent by the Council, why are you here? How did you know I was here?" Eldridge asked.

Simon explained about the museum and the photograph. "Elizabeth grew very attached to Mrs. Eldridge and she's a bit. "

"Of a romantic?"

"I was going to say insane," Simon said with a smile, "but yes, a romantic and she has a fearless streak of altruism that takes us to rather unusual places."

"Like San Francisco in 1906."

132

"Yes," Simon said. "And here. Although we didn't know about the Shard at the time."

"I'm sorry you're mixed up in it now. If it were anything else…"

"If it were anything else, Elizabeth would still find a way to go where angels fear to tread. It's her nature." Simon's heart ached with worry for her. He tried not to think about what unknown risk she might be facing right now. With an effort, he pushed that thought away and took refuge in focusing on the matter at hand. "If you were sent to observe the Shard, how did you end up hiding it? I'm far from an expert on matters involving the Council, but I thought interfering with timelines was high on the list of things *not* to do."

"Typically, yes, although small changes happen all the time. Most of the ripples are localized and nothing of any real significance changes," Eldridge said, sounding more sure of himself, stronger with each word. "But, sometimes, a large link in the chain breaks and if things aren't set right, the repercussions can be disastrous. In the original timeline, the Swedes supposedly made the exchange with someone from MI5 and the Shard was tucked safely away somewhere."

"But that's not what happened. The Swedish agents were killed."

"Exactly. I hid the Shard as best I could until I could figure out what to do or until the next eclipse."

"Why didn't you take it to MI5?"

"MI5 operatives were the ones who killed the Swedes. Maybe it was Nazis who'd managed to infiltrate the section. I don't know. No one else knew about the exchange."

"Blake said MI5 has a mole."

Eldridge shifted in his seat and fixed Simon with an austere expression. "You can't afford to trust anyone. Not with the Shard."

And yet, Simon thought, he'd trusted those men with Elizabeth. Anxiety pulsed through him. He needed to get back to her.

"I went to Charing Cross and hid it in the book box," Eldridge continued. "The next thing I remember is waking up in the hospital."

"And you pretended to have amnesia?"

"Not at first. My memory is vague on far too many things. I do remember the feeling of hearing Elizabeth mention my wife's name." Eldridge paused and cleared his throat. "I can't describe it."

Simon couldn't imagine what that must have been like and prayed he would never know.

"Where is she?" Eldridge said. "Elizabeth. Are we meeting her in Hastings?"

"No. Assuming they escaped without incident," Simon said, his mind overflowing with the unthinkable, "I'll be meeting her later, once you're settled."

"Good. I'm sure she's fine."

"Yes," Simon said. She sure as hell better be.

The drive to Hastings, which normally would have taken an hour and a half, took nearly four. They'd managed to avoid any roadblocks where questions might have been awkward to answer. Judging from the emptiness of the turnpike behind them, Simon was certain they hadn't been followed. He turned off the lane and onto a rutted country road. It hadn't been used in over a year and he had to struggle to keep the wheel straight. If he hadn't known each quirk and curve, he would have plowed into a tree. But this was a path he knew well.

His Great Aunt's cottage was nearly exactly as it was when he'd shown it to Elizabeth when they'd first arrived in England. A little less overgrown perhaps, but otherwise, it was remarkable how little it had changed in so many years. Sebastian was overseas fighting in the war and no one else would be on the grounds. It was the perfect place to leave Eldridge while they looked for the Shard.

He lifted up the edge of the small green pot near the side window where she kept her key. He'd toyed with the idea of playing inside the cottage as a boy, but he'd never dared go inside before.

Eldridge slowly got out of the car. His mind was obviously healing faster than his body. He was still quite weak and Simon worried if he'd be able to manage on his own. He helped Eldridge walk to the cottage.

"I'm all right," Eldridge said in protest, but his grip on Simon's arm told a different story entirely.

It was dark enough at the end of the lane, but inside the house it was completely pitch black. He lit a match and looked for something to cover the windows with. Even though it was well set back from the main road, the last thing they needed was a visit from the home guard or an air raid warden. Thankfully, Sybil's blackout curtains stood at the ready and Simon pulled them closed. He lit two half-full kerosene lamps and handed one to Eldridge.

The room would have been quaint if it hadn't been so dusty and covered with cobwebs. It wasn't that that gave Simon a chill or the cold night air. It was the needlepoint unfinished on a chair; it was the book on the end table and the inescapable sense of a life abruptly ended.

He lifted his lamp and headed into the small kitchen. "Needs a bit of cleaning," he said, pulling the curtains shut, "but you should be safe here."

"It's fine. Although, I really wish you'd let me come with you."

Simon didn't remind him that he was barely strong enough to hold a lamp. He didn't need to. Eldridge knew; his heart just wouldn't accept it. "We'll feel better knowing you're here safe and recovering."

Eldridge shuffled after him and sat down at the small table in the kitchen. "I just need a little rest."

"This is the perfect place for that. Country air and quiet."

135

Simon opened a few cabinets. There were tins of flour, sugar and oats. "I'm not sure any of this is good anymore."

The lid to the flour tin was difficult to remove. "Looks all right." He refastened the lid and put the tin back on the shelf. "There are some canned goods that should still be edible. There should be markets in the village with anything else you might need. No rationed goods, I'm afraid. I'll leave some money here. They'll be quite suspicious of a stranger. Do what you can not to draw attention to yourself and stay close to the cottage as much as possible."

Resigned to his fate, Eldridge nodded. "I understand."

"We won't be long. If this man has the book, we'll get it."

Eldridge didn't say what they were both thinking. And if he doesn't...

"I'll help you make a fire. There's nothing to be done for the smoke, we'll just have to hope no one notices. There's firewood by the hearth and more in a shed around back."

Simon stood uneasily looking around the room. He was sure there was something important he was forgetting.

Eldridge pushed himself up. "I'll be fine. Thank you." He held out his hand and when Simon took it he clasped his other hand over Simon's. "And Godspeed."

By the time Simon left the cottage it was going on two o'clock in the morning. His back ached from driving for so long and his eyes were heavy with lack of sleep, but he drove on. Ever since he and Elizabeth had left each other in front of the hotel he'd had a growing sense of unease. He'd chalked it up to the danger of the rescue, being separated from Elizabeth, but as dawn broke, the niggling feeling that something was wrong grew.

He could not get back to Elizabeth quickly enough.

CHAPTER SEVENTEEN

ELIZABETH HEARD THE FOOTSTEPS coming down the hall. She'd heard four sets of them since she'd gone to bed and each time she'd hoped they were Simon's, she'd been disappointed. This time though, the footsteps stopped outside her door. A vague shadow blocked out the only light in her room, the sliver of warmth that came under the door from the hall. She heard the person on the other side try the doorknob. This must be Simon, she thought and sprang out of bed. She was almost at the door when she realized it could be someone else. It could be one of the spies and she was about to throw open the door.

She scanned the darkness for a weapon. She couldn't see a darn thing, but she mentally recreated the room. The lamp was too big, the chair too heavy. The doorknob jiggled again and she grabbed the first thing she could think of and jumped on the chair ready to strike just as the door opened.

Light from the hall flooded the dark room and a tall shadow stretched out like a grotesque specter. She raised her arm to bludgeon the intruder when she heard the whisper in the dark she'd been waiting for.

"Elizabeth…"

"Oh, Simon," she said, sagging with relief. Thank God.

He turned and flipped on the light. His face sped from concern to amusement in rapid succession. "What are you doing up there?"

"I thought you might be one of the bad guys."

"And so you were going to…rrstart a pillow fight?" His eyes fell on the floppy down pillow in her right hand.

"Well…"

He laughed, relieved, and closed the door. Putting his hands around her waist, he lifted her off the chair and back onto the floor. He held her for a moment and kissed her and Elizabeth relaxed into it. "Are you all right?"

"Everything went according to plan on our end. And you? And Evan? How is he?" Elizabeth tossed the pillow back onto the bed.

"He's weak and his memories are erratic, but he'll be fine, I think."

"Good." She took a closer look at Simon and noticed his eyes were bloodshot and his shoulders slightly hunched. "You must be exhausted. Let's try to get some sleep."

"I could use a good night's sleep," Simon said and then added in a voice so quiet she had to strain to hear. "We need to leave. Now."

She hadn't expected that, but nodded. She was pooped and he was super-pooped, but if Simon said they needed to go, they needed to go. She gathered her clothes and made small talk in case the room was bugged.

"I know what you mean," she said as she dressed. "I'm so tired. The excitement of the day, I guess."

"It has been a long one."

"It was kind of thrilling though, wasn't it?" she said as she scribbled a quick note. "All cloak and dagger."

"Cloaks are fine; it's the daggers I can do without." Simon grabbed her purse from the table and handed it to her. "Try to get some sleep, darling."

They shut off the light and stood in the darkness for a minute before Simon carefully opened the door and they slipped out into the hall. Downstairs, the hotel desk clerk snored into his Beano comic book and Simon and Elizabeth slipped past unnoticed. Simon had parked the car down the lane and they hurried toward it through the early morning chill.

"You didn't tell the others about Cirencester?" Simon asked.

"Nope. I followed the plan." They'd agreed not to let on that they knew anymore than Jack or Blake.

"Good," Simon said. "With a mole in MI5, we can't afford to trust anyone. Not even men who've saved our lives," he added before she could protest. "What if one of them or both is compromised in some way and by leading them to the Shard, we're virtually delivering it to Hitler ourselves?"

It made sense. She didn't want it to and she tried to poke holes in it, but Blake himself had said there was a mole. They couldn't risk letting anyone know where they were going and what they were looking for.

When they arrived at the car, Elizabeth started for the driver's side before remembering everything was reversed in England. "At least we have a car."

"Only for a few more miles," Simon said as he started it. "We're low on petrol and with rations being so tightly controlled, we've no way to buy more. We'll have to do without the car."

Simon drove them to the train station. By the time they got there, the sun was just beginning to rise. He bought two tickets on the first train to Dover. Elizabeth didn't know much about the geography of England, but she was fairly certain Dover was the wrong direction. And not only had Simon bought the tickets, he'd argued with the man in the ticket booth about his change being wrong.

Simon continued to complain about the shoddy service as he led Elizabeth to the small cafe that was just opening its doors. Other early morning travelers crowded the steps out front ready for a hot cup of tea to begin their day. The idea of warm tea was heavenly, but it wasn't meant to be as Simon apparently had other ideas. He helped her through the crowd and she saw him toss their tickets into a waste bin. "This way," he said.

They left the shop sans tea and started down the street away from the station. The morning fog was thick and cold. "The train's back that way," Elizabeth said.

"Yes, but we're taking the bus. Which is this way."

"Sneaky." He'd laid a false trail for Jack and Blake to follow. That explained his mini-scene with the ticket man as well. "You're rather crafty when you want to be, Mr. Cross."

Simon tried to smile slyly, but it was ruined by a titanic yawn. "You should see me when I'm awake."

Elizabeth leaned into his side and they meandered down the street toward the bus station. They had just enough time for a piece of wholemeal toast and a cup of tea before the bus for London arrived.

Blake checked his watch for the second time in ten minutes. He put down his teacup and frowned across the table at Jack. The hotel restaurant buzzed with morning travelers.

"They're newlyweds," Jack said. The clerk had told them that Cross had arrived in the middle of the night and gone straight up to join her. He'd argued to let Elizabeth and Simon sleep in a little.

"This is no time for sentiment," Blake said.

"If not now, when?"

"When the war is over."

"Party pooper." Jack drank down the last drops of his ridiculously expensive cup of coffee. "All right."

They paid the check and went upstairs to Elizabeth's room. Blake knocked on Elizabeth's door, but no answer came.

"I'll get the clerk," Blake said irritated.

"Keep your shorts on," Jack said as he pulled out a small leather case and proceeded to pick the door's lock with ease.

"Very good. What other hidden talents do you have?"

Jack grinned and pushed open the door. "You'll have to ask the girls at Vassar."

Blake snorted in disgust.

The room was empty. He wasn't sure if he was hurt that Elizabeth hadn't trusted him or impressed that she'd had the good sense not to.

"Perfect," Blake said putting his hands on his hips and looked around the room in frustration. He let his hands fall to his sides and then shoved them into his pockets. "What am I going to tell Mother?"

"You can tell him it was my fault, if you want."

"Don't think I won't," Blake said.

While Blake pouted, which he did with great skill, Jack looked around the room for some clue as to where they'd gone. Blake was a good agent, but he worried far too much about what the higher ups thought. Jack had learned early on that what the suits thought didn't amount to a hill of beans as long as you got the job the done. What fun was it if he couldn't improvise a little along the way? Although, partnering with two civilians to break out a high security asset and losing them all was a great way to get *his* asset in a sling.

He scanned the room, knowing he wouldn't find anything useful, when he noticed a note addressed to him on the table.

Sorry for the curveball. Elizabeth

"What's so funny?"

Jack tucked the note into his pocket. "Inside joke."

"Isn't that lovely? We risk our bloody necks and she writes you a joke."

"Aw, come on, Andy."

"Andrew!"

"Sorry. I'm gonna go snoop around a little. They're amateurs. They probably left a trail a mile wide." Although he suspected they were going to be more difficult to find than he let on. They might be new, but they were smart.

"I'm beginning to think we're the amateurs." Blake waved his hand. "Fine, you go ahead. I've got unpleasant calls to make."

"Give Mother my love."

Simon and Elizabeth took the bus to Paddington Station where they boarded a train for Swindon. As confident as they could be that they'd given Blake and Jack the slip and that the rest of the spy brigade had no idea where they were, they let themselves relax a little. That was another thing she was learning, to find moments where she could catch her breath and recoup, even if those moments were fleeting.

Simon purchased the tickets for the journey. They walked the length of the platform as military men in every imaginable uniform filled the second and third class cars. Finally, they reached the first class car and Simon opened the door to their compartment. They shared their tiny room with an elderly nanny and a young boy of about four. The train had hardly left the station when the boy went off down the corridor to explore. A few minutes later, he was duck-walked back into the compartment by a very officious looking ticket inspector.

"Seems Edward's got away again, Mrs. Thompkins," the man said as he planted the little boy in his seat. "We've talked about this before. Can't have him wandering the corridors. He makes faces at the other passengers through the glass. Unpleasant faces."

"I'm sorry," Mrs. Thompkins said as she pinched Edward who stuck out his lower lip in indignation. "He won't do it again."

The inspector nodded and left.

Edward scrunched his face up and squirmed. He pointed toward the netting that was stretched above the seats to create a shelf for luggage.

"I'm sorry to bother you," Mrs. Thompkins said to Simon, "but would you mind?"

"Up there? Are you sure that's safe?"

"He'll be fine and if we're lucky, he'll sleep."

Child safety had a long way to go, but Simon relented.

He picked up the boy and lifted him toward the netting. Edward rolled into it like a hammock and then pushed himself up onto his elbow. "Sweets?" he said putting out a grubby little hand in hope.

"Sorry," Simon said. "I'm afraid I don't have any."

The boy made a sour face and flopped onto his back. Another little face popped up at the disturbance. His sister had been asleep in the net the whole time. She rubbed her eye with a chubby little fist and smiled at Simon. "Hullo."

"Well, hello."

She studied him through sleepy eyes and then put her head back down. "I like your face."

Elizabeth couldn't agree more.

"Thank you," Simon said, bemused, as he sat back down. He smiled up at the little girl. "I like yours too. Very much."

Elizabeth snuggled into his side and rested her head on his shoulder. "Little Zog will be one lucky little girl," she murmured and then let the train rock her into a dreamless sleep.

They arrived in Swindon just past two, said their goodbyes to the children and transferred to the small train up to Cirencester. The Cirencester station was something straight out of an old movie. The entire station consisted of two old brick buildings and a short covered platform. The man working the station shuffled toward them to collect their tickets.

"Do you know where Professor Morley lives?" Simon asked.

The man squinted at Simon and then at Elizabeth.

Simon pressed on. "Would you mind? I'm a colleague from London and I seem to have misplaced his address?"

The station man pursed his lips. The phone in his booth rang and he held up a crooked finger as he walked away.

"Up past the church," another man said. He'd been leaning against the station wall and limped over on a single wooden crutch. "Right on Whiteway. Can't miss it. Just look for the birds."

"The birds?" Simon repeated.

"Can't miss them."

"Thank you," Elizabeth said and then nudged Simon. He dug into his pocket and handed the old soldier a coin.

"Thanks, guv," the man said with a tip of his cap. "Thank you."

As they left the station, Elizabeth noticed a water spigot. "One sec."

She splashed water on her face and gave her teeth a quick finger brushing while Simon watched with amusement.

"Better?"

Her eyes were still scratchy from lack of sleep and she felt mildly sick to her stomach thanks to the train, but otherwise… "Marginally human."

Simon took a quick drink and they walked up the main road into town. The countryside was the definition of idyllic. Lush green pastures on rolling hills with dark copses of trees. There were even small herds of sheep with cream-colored coats of long curly wool.

"What's this area called?"

"This is the Cotswolds. Lovely, isn't it? This area was actually the second largest Roman settlement in Britain. You'll notice how straight some of the roads are. Courtesy of the Roman empire, roughly two thousand years ago."

"That's amazing." Elizabeth slipped her arm into Simon's.

"There are other ruins, even an amphitheater. It's an area rich in archaeology. Take Tar Barrow over there. Many people think it's haunted."

Elizabeth smiled. "You know I love a good ghost story."

Simon patted her hand, humoring her. "We have enough on our plates. No need to pull in ghosts as well."

"We'll come back," she said with a nod. "When we get back."

They passed the church, which was a mere 900 years old, just a medieval baby, and turned onto Whiteway. It wasn't long before they heard the birds. Scores of them flew in and out of trees surrounding a large honey-colored stone house. A flock of Tufted

Ducks came in for a landing near the shore of a small pond. It was beautiful and a little creepy.

They walked up the gravel drive to the house and rang the bell. A heavyset woman answered the door and quickly dried her hands on her flowered apron. "Yes?"

"We're here to see Professor Morley," Simon said.

The woman frowned. "He's busy at the moment. Can you come back another time?"

"We've come an awful long way to see him," Elizabeth said.

Immediately the woman's face brightened. "You're the American. You're late. He's been waiting for you."

CHAPTER EIGHTEEN

PROFESSOR MORLEY'S HOUSEKEEPER USHERED a very confused and slightly suspicious Simon and Elizabeth into the house. How could he possibly have been expecting them? The housekeeper rapped smartly on a dark oak door. "Professor Morley," she said and, without waiting for an answer, opened it and went inside. "Professor?"

A portly man in his mid-sixties sat behind an enormous desk, hunched over a book. He popped a piece of orange into his mouth and answered her without looking up. "How many times have I told you not to bother me when I'm reading, Mrs. Quick?"

"You're always reading," she countered. "And besides your American's here."

The professor looked up and gave Simon and Elizabeth a cursory glance before looking behind them. "Where?"

"Right there," Mrs. Quick said nodding toward Elizabeth.

"My dear woman," the professor said as he wiped his mouth with a white cloth napkin. He pushed himself back from his desk, stood and closed in on them. "Does this girl look like a man from the Appalachian mountains of Alabama to you? If so, you need a rather long rest and if not, you've completely wasted my time."

"It's our fault," Elizabeth said, her mouth watering at the sight of the orange. It was the first piece of fresh fruit she'd seen since they'd gone back in time. "We wanted to see you."

"And so you have. Good day," he waved a dismissive hand and started back to his desk.

"Please," Elizabeth said. "We just need a few minutes of your time."

He turned around slowly and narrowed his eyes. His wild, bushy eyebrows nearly knit together.

"Please," Simon said with wafer thin patience.

Morley held up a silencing hand. "Shh. Say that again, girl."

Elizabeth hesitated. "We just need a few minutes of your time."

"Texas, yes? Tell me I'm right! Wait. North Texas."

"Lubbock. Right." She'd forgotten he was a linguist.

"That's quite impressive, but—" Simon started.

"Sussex," he said to Simon. "Eton and Oxford. Staggeringly dull. UPR. Thoroughly tiresome accent except, in your case, the way your time in America has bastardized it makes it of marginal interest."

"Now, see here—"

"Professor," Elizabeth said, trying to head off whatever chest puffery was about to take place. "I'm sorry I'm not the right American. But we really have come a long way. We're here to see you about a book."

"A book? Oh. Why didn't you say so in the first place?" His face lit up. "Which one? *Centring Dipthongs of Non-Rhotic Accents* or *Intervocalic Alveolar-Flapping and You?*"

"I'm sorry," Elizabeth said. "We met with Professor Giles in London and he said he'd given you a book for your birthday."

"*The Book of Iona*," Simon said.

Morley's face dropped. "Oh, yes, that. I thought you meant one of mine. Giles has never had very good taste in books."

"No," Elizabeth agreed quickly, hoping to win him over. "You don't still have it, do you?"

"Alas no. It and several other volumes of little consequence but, I must say, substantial value were donated to a worthy cause. We all have to do our part, you know."

"Very noble," Simon said between gritted teeth. Obviously, he'd noticed the crate of oranges, box of SPAM and other black market goods piled up behind the professor's desk.

"I'm sure they appreciated your generosity," Elizabeth said hoping to salvage their trip. "It was very kind of you to part with them."

"Yes," Morley said with a put-upon sigh. "They should bring a good price. Put the Spitfire Fund over the top."

With a little coaxing, she might be able to get more out of him. "Is the Spitfire Fund event here in town?"

"No, no. This is over in Bath. A fundraiser tomorrow night, I think. I don't like to get too involved in things locally, you understand. Once people sense you're blessed with a generous nature, they take advantage."

"I'm sure they do," Simon said.

Elizabeth put a comforting hand on Simon's arm. Lack of sleep was making him crankier than usual. "Thank you for your time, Professor."

Elizabeth led Simon out of the office and back onto the street before he could make a scene.

"Idiot," Simon grumbled.

Elizabeth arched an eyebrow.

"Not the accent. I don't care about that. But did you see all of the black market goods? I would very much have liked to have shoved that damn orange down his damn throat."

Elizabeth patted his arm. "You're sweet."

Simon snorted. "That wasn't exactly what I was going for."

She hadn't gotten exactly what she'd hoped for either, but they had found another piece of the puzzle. They hadn't come away entirely empty-handed.

"Come on," Elizabeth said as she slipped her arm through his. "Off to Bath? How far away is it?"

"A few hours by train."

It had been nearly thirty-six hours since either of them had truly slept. The adrenaline from the escape had long worn off, and left her feeling wrung out like an old washcloth fraying at the edges. But, this wasn't a vacation, and considering what other people endured during the war, the least she could do was suck it up. She tried her best to hide just how tired she was and plastered on a smile "Right."

By the time they'd walked back into the center of town, dark clouds had filled the late afternoon sky. The weather had been so cooperative, so temperate, she'd completely forgotten about it until a big fat raindrop splattered across the bridge of her nose. Like an idiot, she looked up and promptly got another one right in the eye.

Simon took her arm and helped her over the now slippery brick pavers and into the shelter of a covered doorway. They huddled together as the skies overhead opened up and the rain came down with a fury. People on the street pulled out umbrellas or shielded their heads as best they could and hurried for cover. Across the street, a mother dragged her son down the sidewalk. He kept his head tilted back and his tongue out to catch the drops.

"Wow," Elizabeth said. "Hello, Mother Nature."

"Wait here." Simon turned up the collar of his coat and pulled down the brim of his hat. He stepped out into the rain and jogged down the street.

A few minutes later, he reappeared. "Here." He took off his hat, shook the water from it and set it on top of her head. He laughed as he pulled it down and it covered her eyes. "There's a pub just down the road. We can dry out there and get something to eat."

Elizabeth pushed the brim of the hat back so she could see and held out her hand.

"Ready?" Simon asked and on her nod they dashed into the rain and ran down the empty street.

The King's Head Inn was dark and wonderfully warm and cozy. A few small wooden tables with a variety of benches and chairs were tucked into nooks or gathered around a large fireplace where a man was busy building a fire.

"I be right with ya," he said.

Simon and Elizabeth took off their coats and hat and hung them on a coatrack by the door. Nearly every inch of ceiling and wall space was covered with photographs, newspaper articles and miniature flags.

Elizabeth noticed a chalkboard with today's specials listed. "Oh, I'm starving. Soup sounds good but what's that wonderful smell?"

"Mulled cider, I think," Simon said. "Although—"

"I want."

"I'm not sure that's wise. It will be hard cider and terribly strong," Simon said.

Elizabeth waved off his warning. "Hard, soft, it doesn't matter as long as it's all mulled and cidery."

"Don't say I didn't warn you."

The man finished lighting the fire and Elizabeth immediately went over to warm up.

"This is heaven," she said. "Thank you."

The man nodded and went back around the bar. "Er have to wait till half past for a Scrumpy."

Elizabeth smiled. She'd heard all sorts of English accents so far, but the West Country was her favorite. It was a wonderful mixture of charming lilt and old school pirate.

"Tea for now, please," Simon said. "Two fish and chips, if the kitchen's open."

The man nodded and disappeared into the back.

Elizabeth settled into a table close to the fire and after ordering, Simon joined her. "I'm afraid you'll have to settle for tea for now. Licensing laws. Can't serve alcohol until five-thirty."

"That's all right. This is perfect."

They sipped their tea until the food was up. The fish and chips were greasy and delicious. At five-thirty on the dot, the drinks arrived and so did a handful of locals, including one old man with a bent walking stick and little Jack Russell terrier in tow. He sat down at a table not far from them, tipping his cap in greeting.

Simon walked to the bar to collect their drinks and gave the owner a few coins. "For the gentleman and one for yourself."

The little old man raised his walking stick in a salute as the publican took the coins. "Cheers!"

Elizabeth held the warm cup in both hands and inhaled the sharp aroma of apples and ginger before taking a small sip. It was delicious and she didn't feel the alcohol until she felt the heat building in her chest. Scrumpy was warm and dangerous and wonderful. After a few sips, she already felt a little light-headed.

A few more regulars came in and joined the old man. One of them leaned over to their table and said, "These dirty old sods want to know if you're married."

"I am," Elizabeth said, wiggling her ring finger and eliciting groans from the men. She giggled. "You all are so handsome, surely you've been snatched up."

The old man raised his glass. "Lost me wife in '38."

"I'm sorry," Elizabeth said.

"Every night," he said, "I be praying the old bat don't find me!" The table broke out in roars of laughter.

"Er got a mouth like a forty shilling iron pot!"

Elizabeth and Simon joined in the laughter and listened to the stories the locals spun, but it wasn't too long before she could feel herself slowly beginning to fade away. The warm room, the good food, the strong alcohol, and loss of sleep were finally catching up with her. Simon tugged at her elbow. Elizabeth looked up to see him standing over her. He had their coats folded over one arm and she vaguely wondered when he'd done that.

"I don't want to go," she said in a voice that sounded whiny even to her own ears.

"I've got a room upstairs."

"You did? I love you so much."

"Good, now come on," he said as he helped her stand. The room tilted and swirled in a way that wasn't entirely unpleasant, but seldom ended well. They said their goodnights and made their way up the narrow stairway to their room over the pub. It was small and simple, but Elizabeth didn't care. It had a bed.

She flopped down onto it and nearly bounced back off. The springs were ready for a fight.

"Come here," she said in her best sultry voice. She dutifully ignored the fact that Simon was fighting not to laugh. He sat down on the bed and she pulled him down beside her. She rolled over so that she was leaning on his chest and started to kiss his neck.

"We should get some sleep," he said, but she could feel his heartbeat race as she kissed him and heard his breath catch when she found that one particular spot that always drove him to distraction.

"Mmm-hmm," she said, working her way up to his jaw and back down again.

His hands caressed her back for a moment and then held her close. He was warm and solid and snoring. She pushed herself up to look at him through blurry eyes. Yup. Snoring away.

She was too tired and too tipsy to be insulted, and laid her head back down on his chest. His arms tightened around her and the last she heard was another gale of laughter from the pub downstairs.

CHAPTER NINETEEN

ELIZABETH FELT LIKE SOMEONE had stuffed cotton and straw into her head while she slept—scratchy straw that rubbed against her eyes and heavy, water-soaked cotton to slosh around where her brain used to be. Scrumpy cider was evil. Even after two cups of weak black coffee, it was all she could do to get a little bread and jam down. The publican took pity on her. "Her be needing a bit of the hair of the dog." He pulled out a hip flask and put a splash in her nearly empty coffee cup.

Simon tipped him and Elizabeth wondered if he'd mind if she just curled up on this bench and never moved again. She forced down the whisky or rye or embalming fluid and followed it with a large glass of water chaser. Simon insisted.

They thanked the publican and Simon offered her his hat.

"Is it still raining?" she asked.

"No, it's a beautiful day."

Elizabeth waved it off and ran a hand over her head to smooth down the bedhead that wouldn't go away. She'd run damp fingers through it after she'd taken her head out from under the tap, but she hadn't had the courage to look in the mirror. If she looked even half as bad as she felt, she was better off not knowing it.

"All right," Simon said and opened the pub door.

Light brighter than the surface of the sun ambushed her and nearly knocked her backwards. Simon helped her out onto the street and after a few excruciating minutes her eyes began to adjust. Wordlessly, they walked down to the station. The same old soldier was there, leaning against the ticketing office.

The train wasn't due for over an hour, but the bench wasn't too hard and Simon's shoulder was just right. She watched life in the quiet town go by until the engine pulled into the station. They settled into their first class compartment, this time the only occupants.

While her head was much improved, her stomach wasn't so sure. For his part, Simon looked rested and content. He'd warned her not to drink the Scrumpy and the fact that he wasn't saying 'I told you so' was really just a sneaky way of saying 'I told you so'. She glared across the small compartment at Simon.

"What?" he said.

"You don't have to rub it in."

"I didn't say anything."

"Your face is saying it. It's 'I told you so'ing' all over the place."

"On behalf of my face, I apologize."

Elizabeth smirked and tilted her head back against the leather seat. She squinted at the luggage netting.

Simon frowned. "Not on your life."

Somewhere past Swindon, Elizabeth started to feel human and by the time they arrived in Bath, she was whole again. The streets of Bath were busy with mid-morning activity. Cars, coaches, army vehicles and lots of bicycles buzzed along the street. As they stood in front of the station trying to formulate a plan, a shoeshine boy latched onto Simon's leg like a hungry animal.

"Shine, Sir?" he asked, already having wrangled Simon's foot onto his box.

Simon looked like he was about to protest but must have noticed what she did, the only sadder looking thing than his shoes was the boy. He was pushing all of ten years old. His pale face was streaked with coal like war paint.

The boy worked at a furious pace as if afraid Simon might change his mind at any minute. "You new in town? I knows every-fink what goes on here. What you need?"

Elizabeth silently ticked off her needs: a bath, a comb, a dress she hadn't been wearing for three days, a mysterious piece of Nordic legend that might or might not let Hell reign on earth.

"What we really need is a place to stay," Simon said. "Any recommendations?"

"Oh! Right. Gentleman like you needs a fine place and your lady too. Royal Station. Right across the street. Queen Victoria stayed there, they say."

"That sounds perfect, thank you."

"All done," the boy said as he snapped his towel against the toe of Simon's shoe.

"Thank you." Simon dug into his pockets and put a few coins into the boy's outstretched hand.

His eyes opened wide and Elizabeth could tell he was sure Simon had made a mistake. The boy couldn't bring himself to say it, but he couldn't just run off with too much either.

"It's all right," Simon said. "Just don't spend it all in one place."

The boy tipped his cap twice, grabbed his shoeshine box and took off before Simon could change his mind.

"The Royal?" he said.

"If it's good enough for the Queen…"

It took a strong heart and good reflexes, but they managed to cross the street to the hotel. The lobby was clean and bright and an enormous blue oriental rug covered most of the floor. She couldn't wait to take a bath in Bath, and judging from the looks the clerk gave them, he couldn't wait for her to either.

Their room wasn't enormous, but there was an en suite bath and that was all that mattered. She started to undress and caught sight of herself in the large mirror over the dresser.

"Simon, you need to see this."

"What is it?"

She turned him to look in the mirror and two scraggly creatures looked back. His clothes were wrinkled and dirty and Elizabeth's dress had several small spots on it she couldn't identify. Her hair was still wild and untamed and looked like someone had taken an iron to half of it.

After a moment of what could only be described as stunned silence, Simon ran his hand over two days of stubble. "Good Lord."

She sniffed the air. "I don't know which of us that is, but my eyes are tearing up."

"You bathe," Simon said. "I saw a barber's across the street. I'll pick up some things and be back within the hour."

"What about our clothes?"

"The hotel will see to them." Simon grabbed his hat and headed for the door.

"And what do we wear in the meantime?" she asked.

Simon put on his hat and tugged down the brim. "Just our smiles."

Professor Morley scribbled in his notebook as he listened to a wax record of a woman from Manchester mangle the English language. It was a miracle those people managed to tie their shoes, he thought as he made another notation. This monograph on class and Northern dialects would surely be his greatest triumph. Of course, only a handful of people on the entire surface of the globe would be able to understand it, but esoteric knowledge was the only knowledge worth having.

He popped a cube of SPAM into his mouth and strained to make out the Queen's English in the garbled mess the woman was making of it. He heard the door to his office open.

"Mrs. Quick," he said as he reached for the phonograph needle in frustration. "I have told you not to disturb me while I'm working."

"Mrs. Quick is out," a tall man said. "I let myself in."

"Did you? Impudent. Then you can let yourself out as well."

"I just need the answers to a few questions," the man said.

Professor Morley stared at him in confusion. "Can't you see I'm working?"

"This won't take long, Professor." The man walked over to his desk, as though they were old friends. He perched on the edge of it and picked up a paperweight. "You had visitors yesterday."

"Yes," he said, yanking the paperweight from the man's hand. "What of it? Get off my desk."

"What did they want?" The man smiled, but there was no warmth in it. He stood and walked around to the side of the desk.

Morley's orders for the man to leave died on his lips. He squinted at him. "Say that again."

"What did they want?"

Morley's throat went suddenly dry. "Voiced labiodental fricative. Very mild."

"What's that?"

Carefully, Morley placed his pencil into his notebook and closed it. "Your English is excellent. Where did you learn it? Munich? It is slightly Alemannic. Düsseldorf?"

Morley tried to move his chair back from the desk and stand, but the man shoved him back into his seat.

"What are you doing?" Morely protested.

The man sighed heavily and pulled something from his pocket. The blade made a clicking sound as it slid into place. Everything, even knives have a language.

"What were they looking for?" The pretense was nearly gone. The labiodental fricative "w" becomes "v", the phoneme "th" becomes "z", the consonant devoicing "g" becomes "k". Vat vere zey lookink for? Curious and very, very German.

Professor Morley had never considered himself brave. He was generally regarded as a coward. An assessment he didn't disagree with. He was too old and too fat to fight. He couldn't bear the privations of austerity the way everyone else did. He liked the things he liked and he could afford them, no one was really being hurt by it. Despite how others saw it, dabbling in the market now and again wasn't such a terrible thing. A crate of oranges one way or the other would hardly make a difference to the war. But, coward though he was, he wasn't a traitor. Even he had his limits.

"What did you tell them?"

"The same thing I'm going to tell you. Nothing. Now, get out." His voice sounded so much calmer than he felt.

"Just a simple question," the man said. "A simple answer and I'll be gone."

Morley stuck out his chin defiantly. "No." He could feel his jowls shaking and tried to stop his trembling.

The man's knife dragged along the top of the desk, gouging a long gash in the surface. "You English will see that pride alone cannot sustain you after we have won the war."

The man's knife inched closer to Morley's throat until the tip dug into his neck. He felt a single drop of blood trickle down his skin. "What did they want?"

Morley's eyes went to the photograph on his desk of his late mother. He would be the man she'd always hoped he would be. Even if only for a fleeting moment.

"Very well," the man said. He lowered the knife and cut a large cube of SPAM and stabbed it with the blade. He pushed it into Morley's lips. "Swallow it."

Morley tried to turn away, but the man was too strong and forced it into his mouth. He tried to chew it, but the man held his jaw closed. "Swallow it."

Morley shook his head, but the man moved around behind him, pinched his nose and covered his mouth. He couldn't breathe. His chest heaved with breath that wouldn't come. He tried to swallow, but it was too large. Desperate, he forced himself, but the meat stuck in his throat. Choking.

161

He tried to pry the man's hands from his head. He clawed at them and hit them. He grasped the man's fingers and tried to pull them away, tried to get even a tiny bit of air. Panic welled in his stomach and spread through his body like fire. His chest burned as he convulsed, his body trying to save him from his soul's folly.

He fought as the darkness closed in. He fought as his muscles seized. He fought as the last bit of breath in his body was spent. He fought until he wasn't a coward anymore.

CHAPTER TWENTY

WITH NOTHING TO DO but wait until the evening's fundraiser, Simon and Elizabeth spent the afternoon walking around Bath. It was like walking through two thousand years of history—from the Roman baths to the Royal Crescent and the Circus. Nearly all of it, buildings that had survived hundreds, even thousands, of years, bore fresh scars from the war.

The Baedeker Blitz in the Spring of 1942, well after the original Blitz, was a series of retaliatory bombing runs. Filed under War Stinks: The RAF had conducted raids earlier in the year in Lübeck, famous for its wooden medieval architecture, aimed at demoralizing the civilian population. Not to be outdone, the Germans retaliated by, supposedly, using the Baedeker Tourist Guide to Britain to choose sites not of military significance, but historical and emotional. Bath had been hit hard.

Part of the amazing Georgian Royal Crescent was crushed and set on fire by incendiary bombs. Dozens of homes and other buildings were leveled to the ground. Evidence of the raid was everywhere.

Large coils of barbed wire stretched between sawhorses ran down the middle of the street in front of the Circus and along most of the main thoroughfares. Despite the piles of rubble and the fresh wounds, the city was vibrant and the people went about their daily routines undeterred.

Elizabeth hated to admit it, but part of her had always felt like the British were stuck in the past, reliving glory years of days long past. But now, she understood it, and she didn't blame them one bit. What the people of England endured during the war and the way they'd shouldered their burdens couldn't be taught in a textbook. Mrs. Miniver was a flickering shadow compared to the real thing. It had been so hard to understand what the people of Britain went through. She didn't dare even think about the rest of Europe. There was no doubt Americans suffered as well, but they hadn't had to send their children away to Canada to keep them safe. No foreign armies marched through the streets of New York. The fears and hardships of war weren't echoed in air raid sirens night after night.

Elizabeth looked around the streets of Bath, at the people whose spirit wouldn't be broken, and was humbled by it. There was a selflessness that she wasn't sure even existed anymore. A quiet everyday courage. It was a feeling she would never forget and one she'd call on time and again when the world grew dark.

Simon squeezed her hand and led her past the enormous Abbey and along the Grand Parade. The concourse ran through the center of town, alongside and just above the River Avon. Once they crossed the bridge it was only a few steps down into the park that ran alongside the river. They found an empty bench and sat down as the sun began to set behind Pulteney Bridge.

Simon slipped his arm over Elizabeth's shoulder and kissed the edge of her forehead.

Elizabeth rested her head on his shoulder. "This is nice, isn't it?"

"Perfect."

"The river, the bridge; it's a definite Kodak moment."

"It is, but that isn't what I meant," Simon said. "I meant this. Us. Together."

The butterflies that had been hibernating in Elizabeth's stomach morphed into a squadron of Spitfires. "Our we is better than my me."

Simon cleared his throat. "What I mean to say is. Elizabeth, will you—"

"Show me your papers."

"Will I...what?"

"Papers," the man behind them said again. He walked around in front of them. "ID Cards, if you please?"

Simon looked like he wanted to throttle the warden and Elizabeth would have gladly held the man down while he did. But, Simon merely grunted and handed the warden their papers.

"Long way from home," the man said as he peered at Simon through dirty wire-rimmed spectacles.

"We're just here for the night. Going to the Spitfire Fundraiser."

"Hmm." The warden handed back their papers. "Best move along then. This is no place to be after dark."

"Of course," Simon said in a voice so tightly polite it could have snapped. "Thank you."

With a sigh, Simon held out his hand and helped Elizabeth up. They both nodded to the warden and hurried toward the path to the stairs. By the time they reached the bridge, the sun and the moment were gone.

The walk to Guildhall was quiet. No matter how much Elizabeth wanted to rewind or just tell Simon "yes," she had to find the patience to let him do this in his own time and his own way. So, they both pretended he hadn't just almost proposed. Again. But he had and Elizabeth's heart swelled to match the smile she was trying so desperately to hide. She tried not to think the words "Mrs. Simon Cross" or "Elizabeth West-Cross" or "Elizabeth West, wife of Professor Simon Cross" or "The Professor and Mrs. Cross", but those and a dozen of others clouded her mind.

The Spitfire Fund Gala was held in the main ballroom of one of Bath's gorgeous Georgian buildings. They bought tickets at the door from the ladies manning the entrance on the ground floor, and climbed the grand staircase to the first floor into what felt like an indoor fair. The near part of the room was cordoned off for games and challenges, while the far end served as a dance floor. Big band music gave the elegant room a fun, raucous edge.

Elizabeth's skin prickled with anticipation. The book they'd spent the last few days searching for was here. Somewhere.

"Let me see what I can find out about the auction," Simon said, as he excused himself and went off in search of someone in charge.

Unable to stand still and wait, Elizabeth wandered amongst the small game stalls. There was even a caricature of Hitler without ears and crying like a baby. For merely 5p, people could pin the donkey ears on the Fuhrer. Elizabeth had spent 10p and got him right in the kisser, twice, much to the pleasure of the crowd, before Simon returned.

"We're supposed to look for a Mrs. Abbott." Simon explained as he came to her side. "She's in charge of the auction. They wouldn't tell me anything else."

"Any idea where to start?"

A voice came over the loud speakers and the music faded. "May I have your attention, please?" the woman said. "Over here. Next to the kissing booth! "

Elizabeth stretched onto her tiptoes to see who was talking. A beautiful woman in her early thirties stood on a small makeshift stage and waved to the crowd. "Thank you," she said in a perfect cut-glass accent. "Thank you so much for coming and supporting our boys. I'm Mrs. Abbott."

There was a round of applause from the crowd. "I'm guessing we start there," Elizabeth said.

"I'd like to thank the gentlemen who normally use this lovely historic space for allowing us to usurp it for the evening." She winked at a man in full Naval dress. "And of course, to the ladies auxiliary for their help with the refreshments and the young Americans, where are you?" She scanned the floor.

A small group of US army enlisted men whistled, waved and said things like "over here baby!"

"Right there, yes." She read from a small index card. "From the 1st Battalion, 16th Infantry Regiment, 1st Infantry Division for their help with our many booths."

Another round of applause bubbled up from the crowd.

"Remember, every shilling you donate, every ticket you purchase brings us that much closer to reaching our goals. That much closer to giving our brave troops the tools they need to win this blasted war!"

The room nearly exploded with applause.

"Together we can see this through. I've never been so proud as I am tonight, to be part of Bath. Part of Somerset. Part of England!"

Elizabeth had to hand it to the lady; she was a pro. She waved to the crowd as the applause continued until the music started again and she stepped down.

Elizabeth and Simon walked toward her before they lost her in the crowd. She was even more beautiful up close. Mrs. Abbott's skin was pale and perfect, and her dress actually shimmered. Elizabeth tugged on the collar of her own plain dress. All that could be said for hers was that it was finally clean.

Simon smoothed down his hair and straightened his tie. "Let me handle this." He stepped forward.

Mrs. Abbott made charming small talk and whirled about to accept the adulation of many admirers. She even schmoozed gracefully. "Oh, thank you. Such an important cause. It's the least I can do."

"Mrs. Abbott," Simon said. "Very rousing speech."

"Thank you," she said and was about to spin away and be willowy to someone else, when she did a double take. An actual old-timey movie double take and her engaging smile, engaged fully on Simon. "I don't think I've had the pleasure," she said extending her hand like a drooping flower.

Elizabeth cocked her head slightly to the side, surprised, but not really, at the small stab of jealousy that poked through. Anything for the cause, she reminded herself.

"Forgive me." Simon took her hand gently. "Sir Simon Cross."

He whipped out that title like a...like a person with a title would. Mrs. Abbott's pale gray eyes visibly sparkled at the mere mention of his sir-iness. She took a quick measure of Simon and must have liked how things added up. She slipped her arm into his and without so much as a how do you do, took him off into the crowd.

Elizabeth stood there, mouth open, like a giant pile of dumb. Finally, she managed to snap out of it and trailed after them like a piece of toilet paper stuck to one of their shoes.

He was just trying to get information; that was all. This was just a recon mission. She trusted Simon. It was that snooty vamp she didn't trust. No one had that much going for them without a pact with the devil or a lot of air brushing. Possibly both.

After a few minutes, Simon eased away from her clutches and pulled Elizabeth to the side. "The silent auction won't start until ten. They'll open the viewing room for half an hour before that. I think though," he said with a glance over his shoulder, "with a little work, I could get in early."

Elizabeth crossed her arms over her chest. "I bet you could. Sir Simon."

"Now, Elizabeth—"

She couldn't help it. She was feeling extra stabby. "Don't now Elizabeth me. I saw how she looked at you."

Simon laughed.

Elizabeth put her hands on her hips. Under normal circumstances she didn't consider herself a jealous person, and she wasn't jealous. She wasn't. She was insulted, riled. Simon continued to laugh and Elizabeth rolled her eyes. Oh hell, she was jealous. "It's not funny."

"Trust me, it is," Simon said. "I don't think we've ever been anywhere where some man hasn't hit on you. And for once, the shoe is on the other foot."

"I'd like to ram my foot—"

"Elizabeth!"

"I'm sorry." She was sorry. A little.

Simon smiled and gently touched her cheek. "You've nothing to worry about. Let me see if I can charm her into viewing the items early."

"Just make sure that's all she shows you."

Simon looked around the room and found Mrs. Abbott. "She is quite attractive."

Elizabeth knew he was teasing her, but her petulant gene spliced with jealousy anyway. "Maybe you should take off your wedding ring."

"Oh, no," he said, turning the ring on his finger. "I think it excites her."

"And on that note," Elizabeth said. "I need a drink."

Simon started to say something, but Elizabeth beat him to it. "No scrumpy."

Evan had grown used to the little cottage. It had only been a few days, but it was so charming and peaceful, he'd quickly fallen into a routine and felt quite at home. He felt stronger too. Last night, he'd slept through the night without nightmares for the first time in he couldn't remember how long.

The foodstuffs were mostly edible, but he did venture down into the village earlier that day. He'd done a masterful job of blending in even if he did say so himself and to himself. That was the one thing he missed. Company. While he was in the hospital, he missed Lillian every hour of every day, but his mind was never fully clear. Now that it was, he felt that ache to see her even more keenly.

He tried to remember the day he left, but the memory wouldn't come. All sorts of others slipped into its place. The day he brought Gerald home. The day he proposed. The day he met her. He'd been on assignment in Chicago. It was 1871 and the night before the Great Fire. Together, they'd survived. Now, she was facing that horror again. But this time she was alone.

Why on earth had he left? Now, it seems absurd that he ever left her side, even for a minute. What he wouldn't give to have that chance again.

He stabbed at the fire in the hearth. The poker brought the coals back to life. "Lillian."

A loud knocking on the door made him jump and turn toward it. Damn, it must have been the fire that gave him away. Why was it always the fire?

The knocking came again. "Hello?"

With the poker still in one hand he went to the door. "Who is it?"

"A friend."

"You've got the wrong house."

"No," the man said. "Simon Cross sent me."

Chapter Twenty-One

Elizabeth didn't like it. Didn't like it one teeny tiny, itty bitty bit. Why did Simon and Mrs. Abbott have to look so perfect together, like something out of *Vanity Fair*? They both carried themselves with the easy grace that privilege and excellent breeding gave a person. Elizabeth had a whole lot of neither.

"I'd like to begin her beguine," Elizabeth mumbled as she watched them glide around the dance floor, effortlessly, like they were glued together. It was beautiful, graceful and slightly nauseating. Finally, the song ended and Glenn Miller's *In the Mood* came on. Simon and Mrs. Abbott left the dance floor, heads together, whispering conspiratorially.

The young American servicemen, no older than the incoming freshmen she'd seen every day, hooted and jumped onto the floor. One of them leapt up into the air and came down into a splits that looked so painful, Elizabeth's hamstring twinged in sympathy. He popped right back up though and two of the men began the most raucous, athletic jitterbug she'd ever seen. The crowd parted to give them room and applauded after each wild flip.

The beat was infectious and Elizabeth couldn't stop herself from dancing in place. One of the soldiers saw her and grabbed onto her hand. Before she could protest, he'd pulled her onto the floor. She had no idea what she was doing, but the boys didn't care. They twirled her, swung her around, picked her up and flipped her over their backs. One slung her into the air and another snatched her up. It was all she could do not to fly into the crowd in a wild spin. Somehow, the boys kept her upright and they jitterbugged and lindy hopped until Elizabeth was ready to pass out or the song ended, whichever happened first. Luckily, it was the song that ended and not Elizabeth.

The boys from Company B helped keep her mind off Simon. They were loud and charming and hell-bent for fun. Whoever said US GIs were overpaid, oversexed and over here had it right. Except for the pay part. There wasn't enough money on Earth to pay these boys for what they were about to do. It was horrifying to realize that most of these kids would never see their next birthday. Considering what they were facing, Elizabeth felt ashamed of her selfishness and pettiness earlier. Simon would be fine and they'd do what they had to do to find the Shard.

For over an hour Simon endured Mrs. Abbott's ceaseless innuendos. He'd had his fill of women like her. He had been expected, in fact, to marry a woman who had been very much like her, beautiful but cold and shallow, raised to care about herself above all. He'd given that up when he'd moved to America. Had given up, really, on love of any sort. Until Elizabeth. How he'd rather be holding her than Mrs. Abbott right now. However, circumstances dictated something else and Simon dutifully played his part as the willing lover. Judging from some of the looks he received, it seemed he wouldn't be the only man who'd had the role. She was a rich widow, bored with war and looking for excitement, and, apparently, used to finding it.

When Mrs. Abbott led him into the Aix-en-Provence room, Simon hoped she was going to show him the auction items, but she had something else in mind. It was all he could do to pry her off him and get to the table with the books.

"Wonderful items," he said, barely sidestepping her wandering hand.

"Find anything interesting?" she asked seductively.

"Yes." *The Book of Iona* was there, but the box was gone. They were so close and still so far away. "This volume, there's supposed to be an ornate case. Is it here somewhere?"

"Mr. Watson took care of all the details," she said, leaning against the table, palms flat on the surface, back arched seductively. "Are you really more interested in some stuffy old box than you are in me?"

Simon had to tread carefully. "Of course not. It's just a trifle, but I was hoping to add it to my collection."

"You like to collect things?" she said as she walked her fingers up his chest.

He captured her hand and pulled her against his body. Her eyes went round with surprise and pleasure. "Some things. Is Mr. Watson here?"

"No, he's not one for parties. At home in Glastonbury, I'd imagine." She wrapped her arms around his neck. "But why are we wasting time talking about him when there are much more pleasurable pursuits to be had."

Simon whispered in her ear. "Yes, there are." He let go of her and disentangled her arms from about his neck. "Goodnight, Mrs. Abbott."

He left the room without looking back. There was a small twinge of conscience, but nothing he couldn't live with. She'd been playing just as much a game as he had, and they both knew it. Her recovery was certain.

Simon searched the ballroom from end to end and Elizabeth was nowhere to be found. He was just getting worried when he heard her voice coming from an adjoining room.

Kneeling on the floor with four American soldiers, Elizabeth scooped up a pair of dice. "Little Joe from Kokomo! The point is four!"

"Elizabeth."

"Hi, Simon," she said and pointed to a pile of money on the floor. "Look at all my simoleons. I'm a winnah!"

The soldiers groaned and one even tossed a wad of paper at her.

"Spoil sports," she said with a laugh.

"If you're finished?" Simon said.

"Husband," she said, earning a round of boos from the men. She gathered up her winnings. "Thanks for the loot, boys. Take care of yourselves."

The men said their goodbyes and went back to their game. All Simon could do was shake his head. His dear Elizabeth. Give her lemons and she'd build an entire empire of lemon chiffon. To say that he admired her was the grossest of understatements.

"What? Craps is good clean fun."

Simon ushered her back into the ballroom and Elizabeth stuffed her winnings into the donation jar.

"Did you see the book?"

"Yes, but—"

"I knew there was going to be a but."

"The box wasn't there," Simon said.

"Because that would be too easy."

"I know where it is though," Simon continued with a smile. "However, we can't get there tonight. We'll have to leave early in the morning."

"I guess that means we should hit the hay early too."

"Not quite yet," Simon said. "There's one thing I've been dying to do all evening."

"Pin the tail on Hitler is totally worth the 5p."

"I'm sure it is, but that isn't what I meant." He took her hand and led her to the dance floor. A beautiful slow instrumental started and Simon took Elizabeth into his arms. They easily fell into the rhythm of the music. He held her close, enjoying the feel of her hand in his and the perfect way their bodies eased together.

"What's this song?" she mumbled against his chest, her voice sweet.

"*Moonlight Serenade*, I think."

She stopped swaying and gasped. Simon looked down his chin to see what was the matter.

"The moon," she said, looking up at him. "We missed the eclipse."

Simon nodded. "Two days ago." He'd thought about reminding her of it, but there wasn't really any point in it.

Elizabeth narrowed her blue eyes and tilted her head at him. He could see her playing through all that had happened in those two days. "Why didn't you say anything?"

"Would you have left if I had?"

She shook her head. "Probably not, but what about you?"

"What about me?"

"You have a say in this, too."

"I do?" he said with a smile.

"Yes. What you want matters."

The words almost came unbidden. Simon only wanted one thing, but this wasn't the place to ask for it. Abruptly, he stopped dancing.

"What's wrong?" she asked.

"Nothing." He held out his hand to her. "Come with me?"

She was clearly confused, but she took his hand. "Anywhere."

They retrieved their coats from the cloakroom and Simon led Elizabeth out of the hall and into the night. Most of Bath was asleep and the streets were quiet and empty. Their footsteps echoed along the pavement. He'd spent hours and hours trying to think of the perfect place and he'd been thwarted at every turn. Now he realized that it didn't matter. Only one thing did.

They were in the middle of a bridge over the River Avon when he stopped. Elizabeth looked at him with patience and perhaps a

175

little worry. All of the planning he'd done, the need for everything to be perfect was replaced with a singular truth.

"I don't want to take one more step alone," he said.

Elizabeth nodded. She understood. She always understood.

"You asked me what I wanted," he said. "And there's only one thing in the world I want—to be with you for the rest of my life."

He took both of her hands in his. "Elizabeth West, will you marry me?"

For a brief moment, the world stopped. He held his breath, waiting, hoping, and then Elizabeth nodded, her eyes glistening in the moonlight. "Yes. Oh, yes."

Simon pulled her body to his and kissed her. And it was as close to perfection as he could imagine. When he finally eased away, his heart filled for the first time, he caressed her cheek.

She laughed happily and wiped at her tears. "I had something pithy planned to say when you asked and now I can't remember it."

"Don't worry," Simon said. "You have a lifetime to try."

Neither got much sleep that night. They made love until the early morning and barely managed a few hours sleep before they had to leave. They got up in a dreamy haze and made love again before the real world forced them to join it.

It was all Elizabeth could do not to break into song. Actual song. Her heart was bursting with the secret of their engagement. She'd dreamt so many times of what it would feel like and nothing came close to the reality. She felt lighter than air; if someone didn't tie her down, she might just float away. Simon wasn't as outwardly giddy, but she could tell he felt the same way. He had a happy smugness about him. His eyes sparked with the love and affection of a wonderful secret shared.

The celebration would have to wait though. They were as close to the Shard as they'd ever been. If they could find it and destroy it, they could go back to Evan and then home.

The bus from Bath that morning only took them as far as Wells. From there, they had to find alternative transportation for the final six miles to Glastonbury. Luckily, a local farmer who was returning from delivering his carrots and leeks to Bristol took pity on them and gave them a ride to the edge of town. He told them that Mr. Watson lived in an old estate not far from there.

They walked up a narrow lane with tall hedgerows to the top of a small hill. Elizabeth's shoes occasionally sank into the wet soil and it was slow going. The morning chill started to fade as the sun warmed things up. The occasional and repeated realization that she was engaged was overwhelming. Simon apologized for not having the ring. He'd bought her the diamond solitaire she'd admired in San Francisco, but worried he might lose it here, had left it at home. The big doodle. Elizabeth couldn't have cared less. She was torn between feeling like she'd come out of a cocoon and somehow knowing this was how she'd always felt.

A shaft of sunlight broke through the curtain of trees and hedges and she noticed something that looked like a large monument in the distance. "What's that?"

"Glastonbury Tor," Simon said, "and the remnants of St. Michael's Church."

The ruins didn't look much like a church anymore; more like a single slice of what had been. All that was left was a medieval-looking tower set on the top of a barren hill. "Where the fairy king lives?"

"Some believe so. There's no dearth of legends about the Tor or the rest of Glastonbury, for that matter. From Joseph of Arimathea and the Holy Grail, to Avalon to Gwynn ap Nudd, Lord of the Underworld and King of the Fairies it's a bit of a catchall for mythology."

Elizabeth caught his hand in hers. "Did I mention we are so coming back here when all of this is over?"

"Agreed. A honeymoon perhaps?"

He said it casually, but she saw his expression. He was as near to bursting with excitement as she was. Maybe they could sing a duet at the top of the hill?

Elizabeth leaned into his side and daydreamed about honeymoon suites and hot monkey sex and they trudged up the rest of the hill to Watson's manor house.

Simon rang the bell. When no one came, they tried again. Still no answer.

"His car's here," Elizabeth said.

Simon followed her gaze. "*A* car is here."

Elizabeth hadn't walked all the way up here for nothing. She raised her hand and pounded on the heavy oak door. "Hello?" she called and then turned to Simon. "Maybe he's still asleep."

A few silent moments later, she edged around the side of the house with Simon close behind and peered in the window. What she saw made her heart stutter. "Simon, look."

The curtains to the study were drawn nearly shut, but there was just enough light to see a man tied to a chair that had been knocked over. "Mr. Watson!"

When he didn't move, she knew. They both knew. Mr. Watson was dead. They walked carefully around to the side of the house. The kitchen door was ajar. Elizabeth's stomach tightened into a cold, lead ball.

"Wait here," Simon said.

"Like hell."

Elizabeth followed him inside. The floorboards creaked under their feet. Of course, with all of the pounding on the door and yelling it was doubtful they'd sneak up on anyone now.

The door to the study was wide open. They stopped and listened, but there were no sounds at all. Slowly, they inched toward the study. Simon peered behind the door to make sure no one was hiding there. The room was large. An imposing desk was on one side and the grand bay windows they'd looked through on the opposite side. The far wall was lined with shelves that were, or had been, filled with books. Now, they were just empty shelves, their contents strewn all over the oriental carpet. In the middle of it all was Mr. Watson, still lashed to the wooden kitchen chair toppled over on its side.

The smell hit her before they'd even entered the room. It wasn't something she'd ever forget. It was faint now, but she knew it the moment they crossed the threshold—the unmistakable odor of burned human flesh. Elizabeth's mouth clenched shut as the bile rose in the back of her throat.

There was a fireplace to the right of the desk that she hadn't been able to see from the doorway. For a brief moment, she gave in to the hope that the odor was just the remnants of the fire in the hearth that had nearly burned itself out. The embers crackled softly, but she knew that wasn't the case.

"Dear God," Simon whispered as he moved closer to Watson.

When Elizabeth came to his side, she gasped.

Watson's fingers were twisted and broken. A thick pool of blood spread out from the gaping gash where his throat had been slit. And a red and black angry mark puckered on his cheek where he'd been burned. His face was frozen in a rictus of surprise and agony.

Elizabeth felt a wave of nausea and had to turn away. Books and papers littered the floor. Cushions from the sofa were torn open, stuffing ripped out. The fire poker lay discarded on the hearth, tossed aside after it had done its work. What sort of person could do that to another human being?

Simon stood and came to her side. "We need to get out of here."

He stepped toward the door, but Elizabeth's voice stopped him. "No. It's here. It's still here."

"You can't know that."

She couldn't, but she did. She felt it with every part of her being. Mr. Watson had died keeping his secret; she was sure of it. "We have to look. We owe him that at least."

She watched Simon silently argue with himself. Finally, he strode forward. "Ten minutes. Not a moment longer."

Elizabeth nodded and cast another glance at Mr. Watson's burned face. Her stomach lurched again. Would she have been so brave? She pushed down the revulsion and the fear that threatened to overwhelm her and began going through the remnants of the room. It had already been well-searched. All of the cabinets were open, the shelves empty; the contents strewn about the room. If the Shard was here, it wasn't sitting on a shelf.

"What if he hid it somewhere else in the house?" Simon said as he searched the far side of the room.

"Would you?" Something pricked at the back of her mind.

"Probably not."

"Where would you hide it?" Elizabeth asked.

"Assuming he hid it at all."

"He knew it was important; why else would he have taken it and left the book? If he hadn't known what it was, he wouldn't have been…tortured." She tried not to look at the body. "He would have just given it to them."

Simon nodded and looked helplessly around the room. "Old houses like this have all sorts of secret hiding places. We don't have time to search them all."

"Is this house old enough to have a priest hole?" Elizabeth asked. "Like Grey Hall?"

"Yes," Simon said. "I think so." He went back to the book-shelves. "Feel for catches, anything that slides or unhooks."

Elizabeth felt around the edges of the cabinets. She ran her fingers along the seams of wood, working her way toward Simon. There was nothing in the small cabinet and she moved to the large wall. When she reached the middle one, she felt a small piece of wood that wasn't there in the others. She slid it to the side and heard the latch click. Her heart went from a canter to gallop. "Simon?"

He joined her and pushed. The back of the cabinet and the shelves swung inward as one unit into a dark hole in the wall.

"Wow."

Simon found a kerosene lamp on the mantle, lit it and came back to peer into the hole. "Hold this."

She held the lamp as he pushed the cabinet back and put one leg inside the opening. He took the lamp from her and stepped fully inside. He propped the cabinet open and held out a hand to her. "Be careful. There are stairs immediately to my right."

Simon helped her into the priest hole and let the cabinet shut. The air was musty and stale. The lamp lit the cramped chamber in the wall. Simon had to work his shoulders up and down to turn around in the narrow space. "The stairs are just here," he said. "Hold onto my hand."

"Not a problem." Elizabeth said, getting a firm grip.

They walked down the narrow staircase into a rough-hewn alcove. It was cold and damp. The ceiling was low and Simon had to stoop down to keep from hitting his head. He held the lamp out into the tunnel.

Bits of the ceiling had fallen recently. Piles of small rocks littered the floor of the tunnel. Small cascades of dirt rained down from the fissures. Elizabeth felt a shiver crawl up her spine and shook it off. After about twenty feet they came to another chamber. It was empty except for a small wooden chair with an ornate box on it. Druidic symbols were carved into the wood—earth squares and Celtic knots. She'd thought using the *Book of Iona* as a hiding place had been a random choice, but now seeing the box and the ancient symbols of protection on it, she was sure Evan had chosen it carefully. And he'd chosen well. The box had protected the Shard from falling into the wrong hands and now it was their turn.

They knelt next to the chair and Simon held the lamp close. He lifted the lid and inside was something wrapped in a piece of soft leather. After a nervous glance at Simon, Elizabeth picked it up and unwrapped it. Her mouth went dry.

Inside the leather wrapping was a piece of metal no more than three inches across, part of an ancient rune etched into the steel.

It could have been her imagination, but she could have sworn it glowed for an instant. "This is it, isn't it?" she whispered. "This is the Shard."

"Yes," Simon said, covering it up again. "Now let's get the hell out of here."

Elizabeth wasn't about to argue. She folded the leather over the Shard and put it back into the box. Such a small thing held so many lives in the balance. She clutched the box to her chest and followed closely behind Simon as he led them back down the corridor and up the stairs.

Simon helped her through the hole in the wall and back into the study. She looked down at Watson's body and silently promised him that he hadn't died in vain. Simon stepped through the hole.

He blew out the lamp and put it on a table. He nodded toward the box in her arms. "The sooner we can destroy that thing the better."

"I wouldn't do that if I were you." They both spun around toward the voice. Elizabeth's heart lunged into her throat. Andrew Blake stepped into the doorway to the hall. "I'll take that."

Elizabeth clutched the box to her chest. "What are you doing here? How did you find us?"

Blake's face was dull, impassive. He completely ignored the body lying on the floor between them. "Give me the Shard."

Simon and Elizabeth shared a quick glance of concern. They both knew Blake wasn't there to help them. Or anyone except himself. Simon turned back to Blake and narrowed his eyes. "No. I don't think we will."

Blake's lips curved in a cruel smile as he pulled a gun from his pocket and pointed it at Elizabeth. "Think again."

CHAPTER TWENTY-TWO

BLAKE'S GAZE NEVER LEFT Simon and the point of his gun never left Elizabeth. Simon's heart raced as he realized the truth written plainly across Blake's face. He'd tossed aside his mask. No remorse; not even a hint of regret remained, just a cold-blooded murderer.

Simon's stomach dipped with the full realization. "You did this. You killed that man."

"He was very stubborn. And foolish. Let us hope you are not."

Elizabeth's voice quavered as she asked, "How could you do that?"

Blake ignored her. Simon needed to get closer to Elizabeth. He needed to put himself in the path of the gun. He took a small step toward Elizabeth, but Blake took an angry step forward. "Do not move. Step back."

Simon held his hands up in surrender and did as he was ordered. There had to be something he could use as a weapon. The only thing that suited his purpose was the fire poker and it was on the other side of the room. As if he'd sensed Simon's thoughts,

Blake moved further into the room until he stood next to the far edge of Watson's desk, the fireplace just behind him.

"You were the mole the whole time," Elizabeth said.

Blake's eyes darted to Elizabeth and he gave her a deferential nod. "Very good. Yes, I was the mole. It was really a rather elegant plan even if I do say so myself."

"You leaked information and blamed it on the mole," Simon said, working it out in his mind. "You were a hero because you'd found a weakness in their defense, but they never suspected you were that weakness. You cultivated their paranoia and their trust at the same time."

"And yours."

Simon's jaw clenched. "Did you?"

Blake's false smile fell. "Enough. Bring me the Shard."

Elizabeth looked to Simon beseeching him for a plan he didn't have. Simon realized he could get closer to Blake if he took him the box. Maybe he could wrest the gun away from him.

Simon stepped forward to take the box from Elizabeth. "I'll do it."

"No," Blake said. "She will bring it to me. Now," Blake said, waving the gun for emphasis.

Elizabeth gave Simon a helpless look before she carefully stepped around Watson's body and crossed the room to Blake.

"Put the box on the desk. Gently." Elizabeth did as he ordered.

"Now, turn around," Blake said, the gun trained on her as she did. "On your knees."

"No!" Simon said, as he lurched forward.

Blake grabbed Elizabeth by the hair and yanked her head back toward him and pressed the muzzle of the gun under her chin. She cried out in surprise.

"One more step and she's dead!"

Simon's muscles tensed as he froze in mid-step. His entire body vibrated with anger and terror. He caught Elizabeth's eyes for a brief moment and saw her fear and defiance. Simon raised his hands again and stepped back. "Please?"

Blake shoved Elizabeth to her knees and put the muzzle of his gun to the top of her head. "You will stay where you are. Both of you, do you understand?"

Simon's heart clenched at the sight of Elizabeth, head down, hands balled into fists as she kneeled on the floor. Blake could have killed them when they first came out of the priest hole. A man who could torture Watson like that, certainly wouldn't have had any qualms about killing the two of them. That meant only one thing. He needed them alive. For how long and why, Simon didn't know, but it gave him hope. And if there was hope, there was a chance.

"If either of you move," Blake said, "even an inch. I will fire."

He glared at Simon who nodded in understanding.

Blake kept the gun to Elizabeth's head and opened the box with his free hand. He took out the leather bundle and put it down on the desk. Slowly, reverently, he unwrapped the Shard. "My honor is my loyalty."

Simon knew that phrase. It was the motto of the SS. Blake was one of them. All the pieces started to fall into place. Blake had killed Bernhardt, the German, one of his own, most likely because he bungled his mission to get information. Blake had helped them with Evan's escape because he knew they would lead him to the Shard. And they'd done just that.

Blake's attention was completely fixed on the Shard, but there was no way Simon could move without Blake seeing, without him killing Elizabeth.

"Wunderhübsch." Blake stared down at the Shard enraptured. "From the Center of the World the Reich will smite the great dragon. The supreme race shall rule again."

It wasn't political ideology that drove Blake; it was religious fanaticism and with that there was no reasoning.

Blake folded the leather back over the Shard and put it into his coat pocket. "The Ahnenerbe have done their job and now I have done mine. My quest is almost complete."

Simon knew that the Ahnenerbe was the archeological branch of the SS. Their expeditions to find evidence of Nordic races ruling the world and even descending from Gods were well documented. He'd also read that Himmler had a special group of SS agents who thought themselves modern day Knights of the Roundtable, but he'd considered that fiction until now.

"Get up," Blake said to Elizabeth. "Stand by your husband."

Elizabeth got to her feet and hurried past Watson to Simon's side. She was pale and trembling, but alive. Thank God. "Are you all right?" he whispered.

She nodded and they turned back to face Blake.

"You are lucky," Blake said. "And you will remain so if you do as I say."

"What do you want from us?" Simon asked.

Blake kept his gun on them. "From you. She is here to merely ensure your cooperation."

"Cooperation in what?"

"Unless Wells has misinformed me, you are quite knowledge-able in the occult."

"Is he one of you too?" Elizabeth asked, her voice raw and angry.

Blake laughed. "Wells? One of us?" His laughter died. "Puerile American. I should have killed him when I had the chance. Did you know his grandmother was a Jew?"

The contempt in Blake's voice made the hair on the back of Simon's neck stand up. It was one thing to watch documentaries about Nazi atrocities, but something else entirely to be standing face to face with one of the men responsible for them.

Simon felt Elizabeth shudder at his side and he held her closer.

"You disapprove," Blake said. "Don't you see that it is not a matter of ideology, but cleanliness. They are a parasite that must be removed."

Simon squeezed Elizabeth's shoulder to stave off any reply she might have. He could feel her anger and he shared it, but arguing with a madman wasn't going to get them out of this alive.

His gun still trained on them, Blake picked up the handset from the phone with his other hand and dialed. "You will come to understand."

"Yes," he said into the phone. "The flowers have been cut." He listened intently, checked his watch and then continued, "The basket is in the shed. I understand."

Blake hung up and grinned. "We should go. We have an important appointment to keep tonight."

"Where are we going?" Elizabeth asked.

He considered her question and then shrugged. "You will find out soon enough. It is best you understand what is expected of you. Your husband's knowledge of the occult is the only thing keeping you both alive. If you cooperate, you will live to see Germany and serve the Reich."

"And if I don't?" Simon said.

Blake merely glanced at Elizabeth.

Simon felt a wave of nausea. If he helped the Nazis he'd be condemning others to die and if he didn't, Elizabeth would die.

Blake tossed the wooden box that had held the shard into the fireplace. "Outside," he said.

He forced them to walk to his car and made Simon get behind the wheel. He and Elizabeth got into the backseat. "Give me your ring, Cross."

Simon looked down at the wedding band on his finger. It was just a thing. As long as Elizabeth was alive and unhurt nothing else mattered.

"Take it off," Blake ordered. "We don't want to arouse suspicion. If Elizabeth is to be by my side at all times, and she will, she must appear to be my wife and not yours."

Cursing silently, Simon pulled the ring from his finger and handed it to Blake.

Blake forced the ring onto his finger and turned to Elizabeth. "You will be the dutiful wife, do you understand? Stay quiet and do as I say and you might live to see Berlin. It is beautiful in the fall."

"If you think—" Elizabeth started, but Simon interrupted.

"She will. Elizabeth, do as he asks." He could tell she was struggling against her instinct to do something reckless. "Please?"

She lowered her eyes and Blake took that to mean submission, but Simon knew Elizabeth too well. She wasn't the sort to do anything against her will quietly, even if it meant her life.

They took a winding route on the back roads toward Cornwall. After several hours they arrived in a small fishing village and parked along a lane near a small bed and breakfast. Simon started to open his door, but Blake clamped him on the shoulder. "Do not forget our arrangement."

"I haven't forgotten," Simon said. He wasn't about to risk Elizabeth's life. He would play along for now and wait for his opportunity.

"Put the keys under the visor," Blake said and Simon did as he was told.

Blake got them a room and escorted them upstairs, careful to keep Simon in front of him and Elizabeth close to his side at all times. Once in the room, he seated Simon in the wooden desk chair by the window. Using his gun hand as a pointer, Blake had Elizabeth tie Simon's hands and feet with curtain sashes, and then had her do it again until he was satisfied she'd given Simon no chance of escape. Her tearful blue eyes begged Simon for forgiveness as she secured the last sash and stepped away as ordered. He didn't seem to see her as much of a threat. Truth be told, physically she wasn't. Andrew Blake could easily overpower her, and worse. Simon prayed Elizabeth recognized that and wouldn't try to play the hero.

When Simon was secured to his specifications, Blake made himself comfortable. He used the pillows to make a makeshift headboard, and then leaned against them, one foot on the floor and the other stretched across the mattress, the gun resting on his thigh. He watched Elizabeth as she paced the length of the small room.

"You really should rest," he said. "We have a long night ahead of us. In about six hours, a small fishing boat will take us off-shore where we will rendezvous with a glorious U-boat to take us back to Germany. They have been ready and waiting for this moment for many months. It will, with apologies to Mr. Churchill, be our finest hour."

Elizabeth turned to Simon. They only had hours to escape. Once they were on the submarine their lives were forfeit and the Shard would be on its way to Germany. They couldn't let either of those things happen.

Elizabeth grimaced and rubbed her temple as she leaned against the wall.

"Are you all right?" Simon asked.

She smiled weakly, ashamed. "Hunger headache."

For a relatively small woman, Elizabeth had an endless appetite. He couldn't blame her though. They hadn't eaten since last night. That thought gave Simon an idea.

"You need to get her something to eat," he said.

Blake arched an eyebrow. "Do I?"

"Unless you want your *wife* to fall into a coma. Which might be difficult to explain as you carry her to the boat," Simon said.

Simon could tell that Blake was on the hook, all he needed to do was reel him in. "She's hypoglycemic. Low blood sugar. Surely, you've noticed how often she eats. If she doesn't get something soon, she'll pass out."

Elizabeth swooned slightly and even managed to look a little pale. If they could just get Blake to take them downstairs, if they were in public, they might have a chance.

"I'll have food sent up," Blake said.

"Small inns like this don't exactly have room service," Simon said. It was a risk. Everything now was a risk, but he had no choice but to take it. "You have the gun; I'm not going to do something to risk her life. But if you don't do something to help her, now, you're as good as sentencing her to death and you'll find me most uncooperative then."

Blake took measure of Simon's threat and slowly smiled. "I like you."

Simon and Elizabeth exchanged worried glances.

"You understand how the game is played," Blake said. "No simpering, no weakness. You play from a position of strength, even when you don't really have it. Very well. I find I'm a bit hungry myself." He held up the gun. "Best behavior."

The pub was crowded and noisy. Blake and Elizabeth sat on a bench together with their backs to the wall with Simon on the opposite side of the table. The gun was in Blake's right pocket, close to Elizabeth.

Blake ordered three pints of bitter. "To celebrate. A great moment in history."

Neither Elizabeth nor Simon drank to his toast. Blake didn't seem to mind. He seemed almost giddy at the prospect of going back to his homeland and bringing such prizes with him.

The pub didn't have any juice or sugar, but they did have jam and gave Elizabeth a piece of toast with a healthy glob of the stuff. She ate it like her life depended on it.

"Better?" Blake said, sipping his beer.

"Yes, thank you," she said.

Simon watched him carefully, waiting for an opportunity. When the food came, Simon realized what it was. Blake ate as many Europeans do. He held his fork in his left hand and his knife in his right and seldom set either down. Blake had a penchant for resting his right hand, the side with the gun, on the table next to his plate. If Simon could just communicate to Elizabeth what he needed her to do.

Their eyes met over the table and Simon's eyes beseeched her to see more than his worry. She noticed something and cocked her head to the side, but quickly looked back down at her food when Blake turned to her. It took several minutes for Simon to communicate what would have been five words. He couldn't be sure she understood, but she was listening and watching.

Simon changed the grip on his fork briefly, repeatedly, from his natural hold to a knife with the blade down. It looked like a nervous tick, but after a few repetitions, Elizabeth seemed to understand. She mimicked his grip for a split second and then shifted back to normal.

Simon spread his right hand out on the table, palm down, hoping she'd understand. His eyes flicked to Blake's hand and back to his own.

Without much conversation, the meal was nearing its end. Quickly. Too quickly. If she didn't strike now, they'd lose their chance. He silently begged her to move.

Blake rested his right hand to the side of the plate and Simon saw Elizabeth's grip change. With all her might she raised her left hand and stabbed Blake's right with her fork.

"Scheisse!"

Blake pulled the fork out of his hand just as Simon lunged across the table and hit him square in the jaw. Elizabeth tried to grab for the gun, but Blake shoved her aside and she slid off the bench onto the floor. Simon reached over the table and grabbed Blake by both lapels. With one fierce pull, he yanked him out of his seat and dragged him over the table. Dishes crashed to the ground. Simon and Blake fell backwards into a heap on the floor, both struggling for the gun.

Simon managed to roll on top of Blake and pressed his forearm into the other man's neck. Blake tried to shove Simon's arm away and reach for his gun, but Simon grabbed his wrist and pinned it to the floor. With his other arm, Simon used all of his strength, all of his weight to cut off Blake's air supply. Blake's free hand pushed at his face, tried to gouge his eyes and then Simon was swiftly pulled back and lifted to his feet.

Several men in the pub had jumped into the fray and pulled the men apart.

"He's got a gun!" Elizabeth cried, pointing at Blake. "In his coat pocket."

Blake struggled, but the men held firm. One of them reached into Blake's pocket and pulled the gun out.

"I'm MI5," Blake said, a trickle of blood falling from his lip. "He's a spy. He's threatened our children if my wife doesn't play along with his twisted game."

"He's lying," Elizabeth said, coming to Simon's side. "That man is not my husband."

"It's all right, darling," Blake said in a sickly sweet voice. "It'll be all right. Please, you have to believe me. That man is a spy."

No one in the room knew quite what to do or whom to believe when Simon realized how to convince them.

"The rings," Simon said, trying to step forward, but held back by the men still restraining him. "The wedding rings. What do the inscriptions say?"

Startled, Elizabeth looked up at him. She had no idea he'd had them engraved. Thankfully, she kept her surprise to herself.

Blake's mouth twitched.

One of the men holding Blake pulled the ring off his finger and held it up to the light.

"If she's your wife, what's engraved on your rings?" Blake had nothing to say.

"Ours is a love beyond the limits of time," Simon said. "SC. Hers will match but with EC at the end."

"He's right," the man with the ring said. "That's what it says." He turned to Blake. "How is it you didn't know that and he did?"

"It's a trick," Blake said weakly.

"He's a German spy," Elizabeth said. "Didn't any of you hear him cry out?"

A man with an eye-patch who had been sitting at a table nearby stepped forward. "I did. I learned a little German in the last war. When they took my eye. Scheisse, he said. Scheisse." The man glared at Blake and then spat at his feet.

Slowly, the entire bar crowded closer to Blake who looked around anxiously for an exit or an ally. Neither of which he would find.

"A German. Here?"

"Give me ten minutes with him. That's all I ask."

"Wait your turn."

"Gerry scum."

The man with the ring tossed it back to Simon. He slid the ring back onto his finger and took Elizabeth by the elbow. "We should go."

"Wait," Elizabeth said. "He's got something else of ours. In his pocket. It's wrapped in leather."

A man pulled it out and handed it to Elizabeth. "There you are, lass."

"This isn't the end," Blake said.

Simon had waited for this moment. "It is for you."

CHAPTER TWENTY-THREE

IT WAS PAST TWO in the morning when they finally arrived at the cottage in Hastings. Elizabeth had tried to sleep on the way, but couldn't. It wasn't every day she got to fork a Nazi spy.

Every ounce of adrenaline in her body had been spent and she was running on fumes, exhausted, but too tired to sleep. She was stuck in a perpetual twilight where everything had a slightly surreal cast to it. The only thing that felt real was Simon.

She leaned against him as they walked to the cottage. They'd expected Evan to be asleep, but smoke filtered from the chimney and a small sliver of light escaped from the edge of the blackout curtain.

Simon knocked gently before opening the door. "Mr. Eldridge? It's Simon and Elizabeth."

Elizabeth could see a pair of legs half covered with a blanket stretched out on the sofa. "Mr. Eldridge?"

"Not quite," a voice said from behind the door.

Simon and Elizabeth spun around in surprise. Simon's arm raised, his hand balled into a fist as he tried to move her behind him. Elizabeth grabbed a walking stick leaning by the doorway as the man pushed the door closed and stepped out from the shadows.

"Jack?" Elizabeth said. Her eyes fixed on the gun in his hand. She really had had enough of men pointing guns at her.

"Sorry," Jack said and then put the gun back in his shoulder holster. He gave them an appraising look. "You two are wound tight."

Elizabeth let out a long breath. "You have no idea."

"What are you doing here?" Simon said stepping away from Jack and toward the sofa.

Elizabeth let the walking stick slide down her hand and leaned it against the wall. Even though Blake had said he hadn't killed Jack, she was incredibly relieved to see it for herself.

"You look like crap," Jack said with a grin.

"Mr. Eldridge?" Simon said as he eased back the blanket. But it wasn't Evan Eldridge underneath it. It was the Russian spy they'd seen at the hotel, gagged and bound. "What's going on?" Simon demanded. "Where's Eldridge?"

"Relax," Jack said. "He's safe."

"What happened?" Elizabeth asked.

"After you gave us the slip, Blake and I agreed to split up. By the way, loved your note," he said with a smile for Elizabeth. "Anyway, he tried to find your trail and I tried to find Eldridge."

"So you were working with Blake," Simon said angrily.

Jack shrugged. "Yeah, you knew that."

Elizabeth went to Simon's side and put a placating hand on his arm. "I think he means he was working with MI5."

"Well, yeah," Jack said. "What do *you* mean?"

"Blake is the mole," Simon said. "Your partner was an SS officer."

"No," Jack said. "Come on. Andy? On the level? I worked with him for months." Jack waved a dismissive hand.

"You mean he worked *you* for months," Simon said. "Where is Eldridge?"

"He's in London. Safe," Jack said, still trying to process what they'd told him.

"Jack, it's true," Elizabeth said. "Blake tortured a man and then killed him. He would have killed us too."

"You're sure?" Jack said.

"He even said something about your grandmother being Jewish."

Jack's expression shifted from disbelief to anger. Something dark and dangerous settled in his eyes. "That son of a bitch." He closed his hand into a fist and looked for something to hit, but stopped himself. "Where is he?"

"Cornwall," Simon said. "But I don't think he'll be a problem any more. There is something else though. He was planning on taking us to a U-boat off the coast just after dark. It might be too late now, but someone should be notified."

Jack nodded. Elizabeth watched as he worked through every-thing—his anger, the betrayal, his shame at not realizing it. He didn't seem the type of man who often doubted himself or lost. The experience left him reeling a little. "I'm sorry," he said. "I promise you, if I'd known I never would have..."

"I know," Elizabeth said. "He found us just as we found the Shard. It's a long story. I'll tell you later. Add it to our list," Elizabeth said and was happy to see Jack smile even if it didn't touch his eyes.

"You're all right?" Jack asked, his voice rough with regret and concern.

Elizabeth nodded. She would miss Jack when this was all over. They hadn't really spent that much time together, but it definitely felt a little like he was the big brother she'd never had.

Simon gestured to the unconscious Russian. "You were telling us what happened here?"

"It only took a few days for me to find your little hideaway, and if I could...I convinced Eldridge you'd sent me so I moved him back to my suite at St. Ermin's. No one else knows. He'll be safe there," Jack assured them. "So then I came back here, figuring you two had to come back here. But Lushinkov showed up instead. He made a nuisance of himself," Jack said as he rubbed a red spot on his jaw, "and ended up camping on the sofa."

"That all sounds plausible," Simon said. "But after what we've been through I'm not exactly inclined to give anyone the benefit of the doubt."

"I don't blame you," Jack said. "Here." Jack unholstered his gun, spun it on a finger so that it landed flat in his palm. He held it out for Simon to take.

Simon looked at the gun and then Elizabeth. She believed Jack and she could tell from Simon's expression, despite his protests to the contrary, he did too.

"Keep it," Simon said.

Jack turned to Elizabeth. "He always this hot and cold?"

"It's been a long day," Elizabeth said, rubbing the grit of being awake far too long from her eyes. "How far is it to London?"

Simon rolled his shoulders to work out the kinks. "Four hours."

It might as well have been twenty. Simon was as bleary-eyed as Elizabeth.

"I'll drive," Jack said. "You two can catch some shuteye in the back."

Simon frowned, but he was too tired to protest.

"What about ?" Elizabeth asked pointing at the Russian.

"I'll send somebody for him later," Jack said. "He'll be fine. Trust me?"

"Do we have a choice?" Simon said.

Jack clapped him on the shoulder. "You always have a choice."

Sometime after dawn, they arrived back in London and Jack pulled up next to the St. Ermin's hotel. They all got out of the car and stretched after the long ride. Elizabeth had had her fill of country roads and cramped quarters. And Nazis. And surprises. What she wanted was for this to be over, for the white hats to win, and for Evan to receive his just reward. And a bath. A long bath.

"Why don't you go up first," Simon said. "We'll join you in a few minutes. I'd like to talk to Elizabeth in private, if you don't mind."

She'd expected as much. Simon had been giving her looks for the last hour of their trips, and not the fun ones either.

Now, it was Jack's turn to hesitate. Slowly, he nodded. "Fair enough." He started across the street. "How do you like your eggs?"

Simon waited until he was on the far side of the street before turning to Elizabeth. "What do we do if Wells demands the Shard?"

Elizabeth massaged her neck. She'd fallen asleep wonky and her body was making her pay for it. "He won't."

Simon's expression told her exactly what he thought of that sentiment. "That was his mission, wasn't it? To find it and take it back to America?"

That was true. Elizabeth hesitated, weighing her belief in the goodness of man against all the badness they'd seen in the past week. Goodness won by a hair. "Maybe it would be safe there?"

"Are you willing to potentially risk thousands upon thousands of lives on a maybe?"

Well, when he put it that way. "No," she admitted.

"We have to take it back with us to the future," Simon said, lowering his voice. "We can find a way to destroy it there."

"Won't that be changing the timeline though?"

"Technically," Simon admitted.

"Is there an untechnical way to do it? The whole point of this was to put things back the way they were supposed to be, right?"

"Yes," Simon said stretching out the word into two skeptical syllables.

"Then that's what we'll do. Give it to the person who had it when this whole mess started."

"Me?" Evan said.

Jack surged out of his chair. "Him?"

Elizabeth gestured for them both to calm down. "Simon and I agree that it's the right thing to do. It was your—" She almost said "mission", but stopped herself. "Mr. Eldridge, you found the Shard; you should decide what's to be done with it."

Evan frowned. "I'm not sure that's wise."

"I'm with him," Jack said. He rubbed his face in fatigue and frustration. "Look, this isn't finders, keepers. I risked my neck for that thing, for all of you. Let me take it back to the States. It'll be safe there."

"You could always just take it from us," Simon said.

Jack frowned. "Yeah, I could, but I don't want to play it that way." He paced across the room. "Look, I don't know who you people are. Where you come from, who you work for. I just know my gut says to trust you. It's usually right, except for that whole Blake thing; that was a big swing and miss." He stopped pacing and ran a hand through his hair with a sigh. "Still, I've gotten this far trusting my instincts and I'm not gonna stop now. But that doesn't mean I'm just gonna roll over either. That thing needs to be locked up, tight." He jabbed a thumb at his chest. "I can do that."

"I don't know," Evan said. "I need time to think."

"Don't take too long," Jack said, his patience wearing thin. "Blake might be gone, but he's not the only one who wants that thing."

There was a knock on the door. Everyone tensed. "Room service."

Simon frowned.

"I told you I was hungry, but, just in case..." Jack motioned for them to move into the hall and pulled his gun.

Evan, Simon and Elizabeth took shelter in the hall.

"Be right there," Jack said before looking back and gesturing for them to move further out of sight.

They moved back deeper into the hall and listened. Elizabeth heard the door open and then Jack sighing.

"Aw, crud."

CHAPTER TWENTY-FOUR

"PARTY'S OVER." JACK OPENED the door the rest of the way. "Mother's here."

A tall, broad shouldered man with a square jaw and silver hair took off his hat as he entered. "Wells," he said with a Scottish accent. "Must you call me that?"

Three other men followed him into the room. One of them pushed a room service cart.

"That's something anyway," Jack said. "You don't mind if I..." He gestured to one of the silver cloches covering the four plates.

"Not at all," the man said.

Jack took one of the plates and a fork and sat down with it at the table. "You can come out. This is Mother. Also known as Sir David Petrie, Director General of MI5. The Big Cheese."

Simon, Elizabeth and Evan stopped peering around the corner and came into the room.

"Sir David," Simon said.

Elizabeth felt a curtsy coming on, but managed to stop it.

Sir David smiled amiably. "Please, sit."

"You're here for the Shard?" Evan said, looking completely at ease, as if he were talking about new wallpaper.

"Yes, I'm sorry for all you've had to endure, Mr. Eldridge, all of you. But rest assured my country is deeply grateful for your service. And the item will be well looked after."

Jack shoveled a forkful of eggs into his mouth. "How'd you know we had it?"

Sir David took a seat, leaned back in his chair and crossed his legs. "We've been watching all of you for some time. Your hospital stay, Mr. Eldridge, drew the attention of some very important people. It seems that when you were suffering from pneumonia, not only did you say some things in your delirium that, shall we say, aroused our curiosity, but when you had an x-ray taken, it revealed something rather remarkable."

Evan touched his heart.

"There appears to be a small machine with wires attached to your heart. Well, our doctors had never seen anything like it and couldn't make heads or tails of it, but it certainly got everyone's attention. That and your involvement with the Shard were enough for us to grow quite concerned."

"I can imagine," Evan said, leaning back and crossing his legs.

"You were waiting for someone to make contact with him," Elizabeth said. "That's what Blake said."

"Yes, that's true. We were keeping him in the front window, so to speak."

"Did you know he was the mole?" Elizabeth asked. "Blake, I mean."

"We've known for quite some time."

"You could have shared that bit, ya know?" Jack said. "I could have kept a few people alive."

"It was a risk we couldn't take," Sir David said. "We kept close watch over him, but after Cirencester, we lost him, I'm afraid."

Elizabeth tried to make sense of it all. "You were following him following us?"

"In a way. We had a man following Blake, but we also had several operatives watching over you as well. We have dozens of men stationed along the railway lines and in various locations around the country. We gave them orders to keep an eye out for you. The old soldier at the train station in Cirencester. The concierge at the Royal Hotel. We were never far."

"Except when Blake kidnapped us," Simon said.

"Yes, I'm sorry about that," he said, his brow furrowing with regret. "Shortly after he killed Professor Morley—"

Elizabeth gasped. "He killed the professor?"

"Yes, I'm afraid so. After that our man failed to check in. His body was found a few hours ago in the river near Bath."

"If you knew all of this, why didn't you just go get the Shard yourself?" Elizabeth asked. Was anyone in England who they seemed to be? She'd been the Council's pawn and now she was MI5's?

"That was the one piece of information we didn't have. We didn't know the location of the Shard and we couldn't do anything more without revealing to Blake that we were on to him. We let him think he had the upper hand and hoped he would eventually lead us to the rest of his contacts. We needed to dig out the rest of the cancer, you see. Since his…capture last night, we've arrested six men, seized some very important materials and sunk a Nazi submarine."

"And nearly got us killed," Simon said.

Sir David nodded regretfully. "We'd hoped to avoid that, but it was a risk we had to take. I hope you understand, I don't take these things lightly, but in times of war difficult decisions have to be made. I don't like involving civilians in these things, but Hitler has brought the war to our doorstep. Some things can't be avoided. And, I think it's safe to say, you're not quite the average civilians, are you?"

Elizabeth flushed guiltily and cast a nervous glance to Simon who looked completely undisturbed. If she could ever teach him poker, they would make a mint.

Sir David smiled and waved a placating hand. "It's all right. I don't expect you to answer that. Regardless of my personal curiosity, which is piqued by the way, I've been asked by the Home Secretary not to press the matter. You've some very important friends here, it seems. I think the Prime Minister himself might have given the order."

"Churchill?" Evan said slowly and thoughtfully.

Sir David arched an eyebrow. "Unless something drastic has happened, yes. Now, about the Shard."

Jack noticed Simon and Elizabeth's hesitation. "You can trust him. If we can't, our problems are a lot bigger than that thing."

Sir David stood. "I give you my word. It will be safe."

Elizabeth knew he could have just taken it from them. Just like Jack could have. She nodded to Simon. It was the right thing. With some hesitation, Simon handed Sir David the small leather-bound package and she felt a weight lift from her shoulders.

Sir David unwrapped it, studied it for a moment and handed it to one of his men. "Right then. Will you be staying in England long?" he said it as though he were politely asking them about their vacation plans.

Simon replied in kind. "We'd like to return to the States as quickly as possible."

Elizabeth was still a few pages behind. The realization that they'd actually done it, that the Shard was safe and not their responsibility anymore was still sinking in.

"Of course," Sir David said. "If my office can be of service in making arrangements, please contact my secretary." He handed Simon his card. "She'll make sure you arrive home safely."

"Thank you." Simon and Sir David shook hands.

Sir David turned to Jack. "As for you. I'll smooth things over with the Brig. He'll understand."

"That'd be a first," Jack said.

Sir David chuckled and extended his hand. "Well done, Jack."

Jack frowned, but shook his hand. "I'm sure glad you're on our side."

Sir David laughed lightly. "Mr. Eldridge, Mr. and Mrs. Cross, safe journey."

He and his entourage left, and Elizabeth felt at loose ends. After being on the run nearly every minute since they'd arrived, she felt a strange sense of loss now that the Shard was actually safe.

Jack plopped down onto the sofa. "So. Who wants to go to the movies?"

"Maybe later, Jack," Elizabeth said. She looked at Simon. They'd missed the eclipse and there was no telling how long it might be until the next one. She'd been so busy with the here and now, she'd never given much thought to what came next. "What do we do now, Simon?"

"Make arrangements to go home," he said, loosening his tie. "Back to the States, I suppose."

She realized they couldn't exactly talk about things openly with Jack in the room, but going back to the States was probably their best bet. She loved England, but there was still a war on and it would be safer to wait for the eclipse back home, if they could find a way to get there. She was running down the possibilities in her mind when she noticed that Evan was being very quiet. He had that far away look in his eyes again. "Are you all right, Mr. Eldridge?"

His eyes refocused and he turned to her. "I think I know where I left my watch."

"We shoulda gone to the movies," Jack said. "This place gives me the creeps."

"I second that emotion," Elizabeth said.

Simon humphed as he paid for the tickets. "It's just wax. You're the one who wanted to tag along, Wells. I'm sure the Hope movie has seats."

"And miss the excitement?" Jack said. "I don't know much, but I do know if there's action in this city, you three are going to be in the middle of it. And I don't want to miss it."

The only good thing about Madame Tussauds Wax Museum was that it was near Baker Street. However, a visit to Sherlock

Holmes would have to wait for another time. They went inside the museum. It had just opened and they had the place to themselves.

"This way, I think," Evan said.

The wax museum was set up as a series of narrow, themed rooms. The corridors were dark except for the mood lights spotlighting the wax tableau. Some of the figures bore a remarkable resemblance to their real life counterparts. Being so close, but still just off enough was what gave the figures a ghoulish quality that made Elizabeth's skin crawl. They looked real, but they lacked souls. Even the ones that were supposed to be friendly had a macabre feel to them.

It had always amazed her that it had become, and still was, a popular tourist destination and had even sprouted satellite museums all over the world. *Come on, darling; let's go look at the gruesome wax figures with lifeless eyes. Don't forget to bring the kiddies!* The whole thing made her shiver. They couldn't get out soon enough.

They followed Evan from darkened room to darkened room. Elizabeth kept her eyes away from the figures for most of the Chamber of Horrors, but peeked just long enough to see five heads on spikes and a bloody corpse lashed to a torture wheel. She closed her eyes and wished they'd gone to the Bob Hope movie.

"You'd think the war would have given them enough of this," Jack said.

True to form, Simon examined each exhibit for historical inaccuracies and gleefully announced each that he found.

Finally, Evan led them to the main room, the Grand Hall, where most of the historical figures were displayed. It was much larger than the other rooms, perhaps thirty feet across, but just as disturbing and dark. They passed by Napoleon and Richard III, Henry the VIII and Benjamin Franklin until Evan stopped at the figure of Winston Churchill.

"I didn't dream it," he said. "At least, I don't think so. Keep a lookout, will you?"

Luckily, the museum was practically deserted. For the moment, at least, they had the entire hall to themselves. Evan stepped up onto the platform and a loud siren wailed. He froze.

Elizabeth's heart stopped and she reached for Simon's hand.

"It's not him," Jack said. He looked up at the ceiling as though he could see the sky. "Air raid."

Evan reached into Churchill's pocket and pulled out his watch. "Thank you, Prime Minister!"

"Back this way, I think," Jack said and they all followed him. They were almost to the exit of the Grand Hall when the bomb hit. The first explosion shook the floor, the second, third, forth and fifth shook everything else.

Anyone who wasn't thrown to the floor, dived down on to it and took cover as best they could. Elizabeth screamed and Simon pulled her to him. He tucked her head under his chest and covered her with his body. The explosions kept coming, louder and louder, one on top of the other, thunderously loud. The building shuddered with each impact. The interior lights flickered. The figures seemed to appear and disappear in the flashing lights. Another explosion came, very close. The whole world shook. Bits of wall and ceiling tumbled to the floor. Dust rained down. And then, the lights failed and they were plunged into total darkness.

As abruptly as they had begun, the bombs stopped.

Simon's weight on top of her was heavy and still. "Simon?"

Torturous seconds slipped by before he replied, "I'm all right. Are you hurt?"

She shook her head, but realized he couldn't see her. "I'm okay. Mr. Eldridge? Jack?"

She heard groans across the room and then the sound of a match being lit. She saw Jack's face in the circle of light from the small flame. He reached down to Evan and helped him sit up. "We're okay."

Jack stood and gave Evan a hand up. He held the match out into the darkness. "Cluster bomb. Not good."

He and Evan joined Elizabeth and Simon in the center of the room. His match burned itself out and they were in the dark again.

"Wait," Simon said. "Don't light another just yet. Do you smell that?"

Elizabeth sniffed the air. Smoke.

"No, but I hear it," Jack said.

He lit another match and they picked their way over the rubble and fallen figures to where the entry to the Chamber of Horrors was. It was a pile of bricks now, taller than a man. He and Simon removed a few bricks and through small holes in the pile of rubble, red fire glowed. Elizabeth could just see two of the wax heads on spikes. Their faces sloughed off, their hair on fire, and the wax skin dripped down, their faces melting. She recoiled from the sight. It brought back memories she'd tried hard to forget. Panic knotted in her stomach. "Why is there so much fire?"

"Incendiaries," Jack explained. "Also not good."

"There was another door," Simon said. "Back by Oliver Cromwell."

"Who?" Jack said.

"Give me the matches," Simon said.

"Light these," Evan said. He held out two candles. "I don't think King George will mind."

Simon lit them and they walked back across the room to the door by Cromwell. It wasn't blocked.

"Thank heaven," Evan said.

But Simon held up a hand for everyone to wait. He handed Elizabeth the candle and put his free hand against the door. He snatched it back and shook it. "Damn it."

"Are you burned?" Elizabeth said.

"No," he said. "But we can't use that door."

They searched the perimeter for another exit. Fallen wax figures littered the floor like the dead—arms broken off, faces cracked. There were no other doors. Both exits were blocked. The building was on fire, and they were trapped.

Chapter Twenty-Five

SMOKE STARTED TO FILL the room.

Simon handed Elizabeth his handkerchief. "Cover your mouth."

"You should use it," she said, handing it back to him.

"Don't be ridiculous."

Chivalry was great, but she wasn't about to let him choke while she used a filter. A piece of jagged rock lay on the floor at her feet. She knelt down and used the sharp edge to tear the handkerchief in half and handed Simon half.

"Partners, right?" she said.

Reluctantly he took his half and covered his mouth.

Jack soon did the same with his handkerchief and handed Evan the other piece.

"Come on fire brigade," Jack whispered under his breath. He looked up nervously, hopefully.

A loud cracking and popping sound came from one side of the room. Instinctively, Elizabeth took a step away from it.

"Move back," Simon said.

Everyone edged back away from the sound. There was a strange hissing sound and more popping, then a moment of silence. Then, hundreds of pounds of wood and brick mixed with fire fell from the ceiling about twenty feet away. It was like a giant had stuck his foot through the floor above them with a thunderous roar.

The debris crushed Napoleon. An avalanche of fiery embers tumbled down into the room through the hole. The Duke of Wellington shimmered in the heat, caught fire and melted like ice cream in the sun.

Elizabeth squeezed Simon's hand even more tightly as they all moved as far away from the fire as they could. She really did not like fires. She'd almost died in one on King's yacht and since then had developed a healthy aversion to burning alive. As more fire poured into the room, a jolt of panic ran through her body like an electric shock. She had the odd feeling that this was how a horse in a barn-fire felt. She tried to catch her breath, to calm herself down, but the feeling of panic grew.

Even more of the ceiling gave way and the hole in the ceiling across the room grew larger and closer. More fire poured into the Grand Hall. The smoke was getting thicker, darker. The heat from the fire felt like a living thing, pushing against them, shoving them against the far wall.

Elizabeth gripped Simon's arm and felt the leading edge of hysteria in her voice. "Simon?"

He understood. She'd told him about the nightmares. And just as she'd held him what seemed like years ago to comfort him when his nightmares overtook him, he held her now. "We're not finished yet," he said.

"Oh, what I wouldn't do for a little lunar eclipse right about now," Evan said, gripping his watch. Sweat ran down his cheek and the fire reflected off his pale face.

"I was thinking of a nice cold glass of American beer, personally," Jack said.

"The moon." An idea tickled the edge of Elizabeth's mind. In a flash, she realized it had always been there. A bit of knowledge that had nested in the back of her mind. She finally opened the door and let it out.

"The key," she said. She pulled the chain from around her neck that held the small key Teddy had given her as a gift in 1906.

"What about it?" Simon asked.

"I asked Teddy what this was when he gave it to me. He said it was the moon."

Simon looked at her in confusion.

"The *moon*, Simon. It's the watch key."

Understanding, Simon took the key from her.

"Teddy?" Evan said. "That crazy wonderful little man! Do you think...?"

Jack looked at them as if they'd lost their minds. "Who's Teddy?"

Was it really possible that Teddy had created a way for them to travel without an eclipse? The moon was the key and the key was the moon. Another part of the ceiling collapsed and there was no time left to wonder.

Simon hurriedly took out his watch. "Everyone hold hands. If this works, we need to be touching each other."

"What are you talking about?" Jack said. "If what works?"

Elizabeth held out her hand. "You're about to get that cold beer. I hope."

Jack clearly had no idea what she was talking about.

"Trust me," she said.

He nodded and took her hand and grabbed Evan's hand with his other.

Elizabeth gripped Simon's arm.

"No matter what happens," he said.

"As long as we're together."

"Right. Here we go." Simon took a breath and inserted the key into the watch and turned it. Nothing happened. It couldn't end like this. It couldn't. Elizabeth's anxiety reached a fever pitch. She trembled and turned to look at Simon as the fire across the room crawled closer.

And then, Elizabeth felt the familiar tugging sensation deep in her stomach. "Don't let go!"

The electric blue light from the watch mingled with red from the fire and the world around them shook itself apart.

The roaring of the fire and the creaking of the collapsing building were gone in an instant, replaced by the quiet of Sebastian's study and the soft trilling of a songbird outside the window. Elizabeth felt like her entire body was still vibrating at a high frequency. She shivered to shake off the effect.

"Hoo," Evan gasped, summing everyone's feelings. "That was more intense, wasn't it?"

"Yes," Simon said. He put the watch down and turned Elizabeth to face him. "Are you all right?"

She nodded. That was too close for comfort.

Jack stumbled, nearly falling to his knees. He looked pale and squinted with the pain of an instant and crushing headache. "Okay, what just happened?"

Ignoring Jack, Simon leaned down and kissed Elizabeth. She slipped her arms around his shoulders. When they pulled apart she sighed in relief. For a moment there, she really thought they might not make it.

"That's sweet," Jack said in a tone that clearly meant he didn't think so. "Maybe someone could tell me what just happened and where the hell we are?"

"My boy," Evan said, clapping Jack on the shoulder "You've just traveled through time."

Jack looked at Evan as though the old man had finally lost it and then turned to Elizabeth for a better explanation.

"This might be hard for you to believe," she said remembering her first experience, how confused and hung over she'd felt.

"Are we dead?"

"No, we're just—"

Simon poured Jack a drink. "Have you ever read any HG Wells?"

Jack flopped into a chair. "I feel like I went three rounds with Louis. And then had some bad shrimp." He picked up a nearby wastebasket and hugged it like a teddy bear. Despite that, he managed to drink down the scotch Simon had given him in one burning gulp. He grimaced and then looked up at them. "Okay, so what's this time travel thing?"

They spent the next half hour explaining time travel to Jack. Like everything else, he took it in stride. Just another adventure.

"So this is the future?"

"To you," Simon said, "Yes."

He looked around Sebastian's study. "Doesn't look that different."

Elizabeth laughed. "You ain't seen nothin' yet."

"Can I stay? Or do you have to send me back?"

Elizabeth had been so focused on not ending up a pile of ashes she hadn't thought that far ahead. She didn't want to send him back into the middle of a war, but the idea of Jack running lose in the future...There was no telling what sort of trouble he'd get himself into. "I don't know," she finally said.

"We'll discuss that when we get back," Simon said.

"Where are you going?" Jack said, looking mildly alarmed. "You're not going back there, are you?"

"No," Simon said. He smiled at Evan. "We have somewhere else to go."

Relief didn't begin to explain the expression on Evan's face.

"Unless you'd rather go alone," Elizabeth said and took the key out of Simon's watch and held it out to Evan.

"No, that's yours." Evan put the key in her palm and closed her fingers over it. "Hold on tight to it."

"I could wait for an eclipse," Evan said. Elizabeth could see the effort it took to offer that possibility.

"I think you've waited long enough," she said. "I know Lillian has."

Evan's eyes welled with tears. He blinked them away and stood up straighter. "Yes, she has."

Simon adjusted his watch and took back the key.

"We should be back in a few seconds, Jack."

"Seconds?"

"If for some reason, we're not," Elizabeth said as she took Evan's hand. "Try not to destroy the future."

Jack frowned at that and nodded, taking another swig of Scotch.

"When will we arrive?" Evan said.

"A few months after the earthquake," Simon said. "The house survived that, but it was destroyed by the fires. We can only hope she stayed and rebuilt."

"She would. I know she would."

"Hold tight," Simon said and the electric blue light snaked up his arm and the world shifted again.

They arrived in the same location Elizabeth had, in Mrs. Eldridge's garden, but the hedge she'd been so well acquainted with was gone along with the trees and nearly everything else with it. The street corner that had once held some of the most beautiful and luxurious mansions in San Francisco was covered with empty lots and shells of once grand houses. Everything on Nob Hill that had survived the earthquake had been razed by fire. But amongst the ruins, new life was being built. Frames of even grander houses rose out of the barren ground. San Francisco was rising again.

"She did," Evan said in a soft voice.

Elizabeth followed his gaze. The house wasn't quite finished, but it was the same, or it would be. They walked to the newly laid path to the front stoop. Evan stopped before the stairs. He let out a long shuddering breath and nodded for them to go ahead.

Simon knocked on the door. A moment later, it swung open and Gerald filled the doorway. He was wearing his usual expression of annoyance. "Yes? What in God's name? Elizabeth?"

His dour face lit with a broad smile. "It's good to see you, girl. And you too I guess," he added with a glance at Simon.

Elizabeth laughed. How she'd missed this dear man. But her reunions could wait. "Is Mrs. Eldridge here?"

"Lillian. We have visitors!"

"Is it the man come about the garden?" Mrs. Eldridge said, as she came to the door. "Oh, hello, dear. Mr. Cross," she said as if she weren't surprised in the slightest to see them again.

Elizabeth felt her throat tighten with emotion. She smiled and took Mrs. Eldridge's hand. "We brought you something."

She and Simon stepped aside. Evan stood behind them, halfway up the stairs. He took a tentative step.

Mrs. Eldridge's gaze landed on Evan and her composure faltered. She didn't believe her eyes or didn't dare believe them. "Evan?"

Evan took the last few stairs and stood in front of her. "I'm sorry I kept you waiting."

She reached out and touched his chest, testing to see if he was real. Her hand trembled and he covered it with his own and then kissed it. She gasped and cried with joy and he pulled her to him. They held one another, trembling in each other's arms. It was the most beautiful thing Elizabeth had ever seen. The tears that had constricted her throat moments earlier flowed freely now. Evan ducked his head and whispered something to Lillian and she cried harder and he held her tighter.

Simon and Elizabeth shared a glance over the couple. It was a promise and affirmation. Elizabeth wiped the tears from her eyes with the back of her hand. She caught a glimpse of Gerald. He had tears in his eyes too. Joy and, she suspected, a little sadness.

Evan eased Lillian back and kissed her cheek. He saw Gerald and put out his hand. "Gerald, it's good to see. Thank you."

Gerald sniffled in a manly way, cleared his throat and shook Evan's hand. "Good to have you home, sir."

Mr. and Mrs. Eldridge started into the house still in each other's arms. Mrs. Eldridge stopped and turned back. "Thank you. Thank you both so much."

"It was our pleasure," Simon said, taking Elizabeth's hand.

"You will stay, won't you? For a little while? I know Maxwell and Teddy would be sick if they missed you."

"Of course," Elizabeth said, elated at the idea and then looked up to Simon. "We have time, don't we, Simon?"

He squeezed her hand. "All the time in the world."

THE END

NOTE TO THE READERS

Thank you for reading FRAGMENTS; I truly hope you enjoyed reading it as much as I enjoyed writing it.

If you liked it, please consider lending a copy to a friend or posting a short review at http://www.amazon.com/author/moniquemartin

ALSO BY MONIQUE MARTIN

Out of Time: A Time Travel Mystery (Book #1, Out of Time)
When the Walls Fell (Book #2, Out of Time)

ABOUT THE AUTHOR

MONIQUE WAS BORN IN Houston, Texas, but her family soon moved to Southern California. She grew up on both coasts, living in Connecticut and California. She currently resides in Southern California with her naughty Siamese cat, Monkey.

She's currently working on an adaptation of one of her screenplays, several short stories and novels, and the fourth book in the *Out of Time* series.

For news and information about Monique and upcoming releases, please visit: http://moniquemartin.weebly.com/

Turn the page for an excerpt from the first book of the OUT OF TIME series!

An Excerpt From

Out Of Time

The first book of the "Out of Time" series by Monique Martin

CHAPTER ONE

THE NIGHTMARES HAD COME again.
Simon Cross pushed himself off the bed and away from the cold, sweat-soaked sheets. His heart racing, his breath quick and rough, he forced his eyes to adjust to the dark room as the last vestiges of sleep faded.

He glared down at his bed, as if it were to blame, as if the sheets and pillows had knowingly harbored the nightmare. He felt a surge of panic and escaped from the darkened bedroom.

The moon was nearly full and cast its silvery light through the open curtains giving the living room an unearthly glow. Vague shadows stretched out like the taunting specters of his nightmare. Ignoring everything but his destination, he strode to the liquor cabinet. His hands trembled as he poured a stiff Scotch and downed it in one swig. Without pause, he poured another. His hands gripped the crystal glass as he tried in vain to keep it from clattering on the silver tray.

Disgusted with his weakness, he slammed the bottle down and clamped his eyes shut. His hands still trembled.

"Bloody hell."

The last time he'd had a nightmare like this was over thirty years ago. Yet, the memory rang with sharp clarity in his mind. His grandfather. The violence. The blood. And above all, the helplessness.

Simon let out a short burst of breath. He tried to convince himself this had merely been another dream. Another dream about her.

Ignoring the stacks of open boxes littering the floor, he tightened his jaw, grabbed the glass of Scotch and prowled across the room. He'd dreamt of her before. He was, after all, only human. She was attractive, intelligent and everything he wanted, but could never have. It was only natural she'd be in his thoughts. But there was nothing natural about this dream. This nightmare. This wasn't a fool's late night fantasy, brought on by loneliness and assuaged by a cold shower. This was something unspeakable.

Unconsciously, he clenched and unclenched his free hand. No concrete images remained, just an unwavering sense of horror, of an inevitable evil.

Exactly as it had been before.

He took another drink and concentrated on the warm burning sensation as the liquor seeped down into his chest. There was no avoiding the harbinger of his dream. With the certainty only a condemned man can feel, he knew one absolute truth.

Elizabeth West was going to die.

Elizabeth had heard it all before. But no matter how many times she listened to Professor Cross' lectures, she marveled at the way he held the class in the palm of his hand. As always, there wasn't an empty seat in the classroom. Introduction to Occult Studies was a favorite at the University of California Santa Barbara. Most students were there for the excitement of it, the dark abiding thrill of all things supernatural, like attending a semester-long horror movie. A few, like herself, were there for something more.

When she'd taken his class as an undergraduate, floating along in the sea of the undeclared, she had no idea that four years later she'd be his graduate teaching assistant working toward her Masters in Occult Studies. A meandering path through her Humanities requirements had left her still wanting for something. While all the courses were interesting, none of them sparked her interest. Until she happened upon Professor Cross' class.

In retrospect, she wasn't sure if it was the man or the subject that had first drawn her in, and in the end it didn't matter. It had taken persistence and a thick skin to convince him she was serious about becoming his graduate teaching assistant. At first, she didn't understand why he'd tried to dissuade her. After attending one Board of Chancellors' meeting in his stead, she had a pretty good idea. Occult Studies was nothing more than a curiosity in their eyes. The poor foster child of interdepartmental parents, Occult Studies was hardly recognized as a serious area of academia. Technically it fell under the auspices of Folklore and Mythology, but for Professor Cross it was a life's work and something very real. His passion inspired her, in more ways than one.

Elizabeth watched him pace slowly behind the lectern, hypnotizing the class with his fluid movements, setting them up for the kill. His keen eyes scanned the classroom, pulling each student under his spell. When his eyes fell upon her, he paused, almost losing his place. He frowned and continued. No one else noticed the minor lapse, but claxons went off in Elizabeth's mind.

There was something off about him today. His normally squared shoulders were hunched. His sandy brown hair was slightly unkempt as though he'd dragged his fingers through it too many times. She'd noticed that morning he seemed out of sorts, and chalked it up to overwork. But there really wasn't a time when Professor Cross wasn't overworked. Something was definitely wrong. The untrained eye would see only typical Cross—brilliant, terse and otherwise occupied. Elizabeth knew him far too well to believe the simplicity of his façade. Working in close quarters had given her insights into the man that most people never knew. What others saw as detachment, she saw as stoic vulnerability.

On the rare occasion he'd let his guard down, she'd seen the depths of the man inside. She knew nothing could ever come of it. Aside from the twenty year age difference, he listened to Stravinsky, she listened to Sting. He was from South of London, she was from North of Lubbock. He grew up with a silver spoon, she grew up with a spork. It was hopeless. She was used to dreaming about things she could never have. There was no reason to think this was anything different.

Simon walked across the stage, powerfully graceful and deceptively smooth. Elizabeth shifted in her seat and needlessly adjusted her skirt.

Why did he have to be so damn attractive? He was handsome. The overwhelming female enrollment in his class was testimony to that. Tall, a few inches over six feet, slender, but not lanky. Eyes of a deep green, tinged with the sadness of having seen too much of the world. And his voice—a hypnotic, deep baritone with a cut glass English accent. But those weren't the things she'd fallen in love with. It was something else, something gentle beneath the hard edge, something needful beneath the control.

"And unlike the overly sentimentalized versions of vampires we see in today's media," Professor Cross said, his voice dripping with sarcasm. "Calmet's writings spoke to the truth of the beast. An unyielding malevolence." He paused and leaned on the podium. "Purge Tom Cruise from your malleable little minds."

The class snickered, and he waited impatiently for them to settle. "The vampire would suck the blood of the living, so as to make the victim's body fall away visibly to skin and bones. An insatiable hunger that kills without remorse," he said and surveyed the classroom.

Elizabeth knew that look, a forlorn hope of seeing some spark of interest, or God forbid, hear some intelligent discourse on the subject. Instead, a blonde girl sitting in the back row made a sound of disgust.

Professor Cross frowned. "Must you do that every class, Miss Danzler?"

She had the good sense to look chagrined. "Sorry, Professor."

Before he could retort that perhaps she should consider a field of study other than the occult, as Elizabeth knew he would, a handsome, athletic student sitting next to her bared his biceps and chimed in, "Don't worry, baby. These are lethal in all dimensions."

Professor Cross assumed his well-practiced air of indifference. "Failing that, Mr. Andrews, you could always bludgeon the demon to death with your monumental ego."

A wave of stifled laughter traveled across the room. As much as the students enjoyed the dark fascination of Cross' Occult Studies course, they also loved his unrelenting sarcasm. Sometimes, he went too far of course, and Elizabeth was left to smooth down the ruffled feathers.

"Sadly, it appears the only thing thicker than your muscles is your skull."

This was one of those times.

The class ended and the students began to pack up. "Don't forget chapters seventeen and eighteen of Grey's Lycanthropy of Eastern Europe for next week."

Elizabeth left her seat and started toward the back of the classroom. Time for a little damage control.

Professor Cross gathered his notes from the podium and turned to look for his assistant. Miss West had already left her customary front row seat and was climbing the stairs toward the back of the amphitheater.

Simon closed his briefcase with more force than necessary and tried to look away. He frowned at the familiar way Elizabeth touched the young man's forearm. Not that he was jealous. That would be patently absurd. Simon simply didn't suffer fools gladly, even by proxy. His mood soured as Elizabeth said something undoubtedly utterly charming and won a laugh from the hulking imbecile. Simon gritted his teeth and waited impatiently for the scene to come to an end. Elizabeth smiled one last time and headed back down the stairs. He glared at her in greeting and gestured brusquely that they should leave.

His mood still sour, Simon opened the classroom door and held it for her. Elizabeth smiled her thanks and walked out into the corridor. He followed her out, moving quickly down the crowded hall, keeping his strides long, forcing her to almost jog to keep up. After a few moments of tense silence, he stopped abruptly and turned to glare down at her.

"I don't need a nursemaid, Miss West."

Elizabeth cocked her head to the side and frowned. "That's debatable, but I wasn't—"

Simon arched an eyebrow in disbelief, challenging her to deny it.

"All right, I was."

Simon snorted.

"But you've got to admit you were in rare form, even for you."

"Your point?"

"That a little browbeating goes a long way. Lance is a good guy. He was just showing off."

"For your benefit, I suppose?" Simon said and instantly wished he could take the words back.

Elizabeth laughed. "Hardly. I'm not exactly his type," she said with a rueful, lopsided smile.

He felt an odd urge to comfort her, to tell her Andrews was a simpleton, but the words died in his throat. How did she do that? One moment she was forthright and confident, challenging him; and the next shy and achingly vulnerable.

"Besides," she added. "It'd be unethical to date a student."

That was something he'd told himself daily. He cleared his throat uncomfortably. "Yes, quite right. Well, we have work to do. Shall we?" he said and gestured down the hall.

"No rest for the wicked," she said with a grin and started down the corridor.

Simon watched her disappear into the mass of students and took a deep breath. The scent of her perfume lingered in the air. "None indeed."

Elizabeth set down her pen and massaged her cramping fingers. She could swear she did more work correcting the papers than the students did writing them. And the tiny desk lamp that passed for light in the room was making her eyes cross.

It had taken Professor Cross a year to acquiesce to her request for an actual desk in his office. At first, he'd done everything he could to keep her out of what she liked to call his inner sanctum. He kept the room dark. Suitable, he'd said, for their work. The room was tiny, another testament to the lack of enthusiasm on the part of the Board. He'd been a professor there for nearly ten years and had labored in obscurity. Although, he seemed just as pleased that they left him alone.

Grant money was scarce, if not non-existent, and so he used his own money to further their research. For all the good it did. It seemed the latest get rich quick scheme in the former Soviet Union was the illegal export of so-called occult artifacts—a lock of

genuine Baba Yaga hair or, her personal favorite, werewolf drop-
pings. Capitalism at its best. For all the money spent, not one
thing had been authentic. But Professor Cross was undeterred, and
so their research trudged on.

Elizabeth rubbed her eyes and stole a glimpse of him in the
reflection of the glass covering the Bosch print on the wall, the
only decoration in an otherwise impersonal office. He really did
look tired. More than that, he looked worried. Bent over his desk,
one hand wrapped around his head casting a shadow over his face.

"You look like hell," she said.

Simon's eyes snapped up to meet hers. "Thank you," he said
tartly.

"I just meant… Are you all right?"

Elizabeth steeled herself for his curt reply, but something
stopped him. He looked at her and the hard light in his green eyes
softened. "I'm fine," he said. "Thank you."

Then, as quickly as it had disappeared, his natural aloofness
re-established itself. He indicated the large stack of graded papers
on his desk. "I think that's enough for one night."

Elizabeth shook her head. "I'm okay."

"You can finish the rest tomorrow and drop them off at my
house."

A yawn squelched any protest she was going to make. "All
right. I could use some good sleep for a change. I've been having
this dream. Very David Lynch. Totally and completely unnerving."

Simon dropped his pen and quickly retrieved it. "I see."

Elizabeth shrugged and packed her bag. "I'm gonna sleep like
the dead tonight."

She turned back to say goodnight and found him staring at her
again with the oddest expression on his face. "Are you sure you're
okay?"

He seemed to come back to himself. "Yes, of course. Goodnight,
Miss West."

"Good night, Professor," she said and left the office, her footfalls echoing down the empty hallway.

Simon gripped his pen so tightly his knuckles were white with the strain. The mention of her dream brought back the memory of his nightmare from the last few nights. He'd wanted desperately to ask her about her dream, to tell her about his, but felt too foolish. What could he say? I dreamt about you last night. Don't know any details, but you died a horrible death. Have a good night. Pillock.

He forced himself to put down his pen and pushed away the fresh wave of anxiety that threatened to pull him under. He'd managed for most of the day to forget, to feel safe in having her by his side. He couldn't say anything, but he couldn't let her walk away either. Before he knew it, he was on his feet and hurrying out into the hall. She was nearly at the corner when he caught her. "May I walk you to your car?"

Elizabeth started and then blinked at him in surprise. "I'm right outside," she said pointing to the doorway around the bend. "It's not really far enough for a walking to."

He hadn't expected her to refuse and felt like a schoolboy who'd been turned down for a date. "Yes, well then. Good night, Miss West," he said and turned back toward his office before he could make a bigger fool of himself. He walked into his office and closed the door. The main door to the building closed with a thud, and he put his hand to his forehead. Gibbering dolt. Tongue-tied over a woman half his age.

Moments later, he heard voices outside and looked out his office window. Elizabeth waved goodbye to someone then walked alone into the parking lot.

He watched her through the slats of the louvered blinds. He was used to being on the inside looking out. It was how he lived. The loneliness had become a welcome companion, reinforcing old memories and keeping him safe from new ones.

He scanned the darkness for unseen dangers, but the night was quiet and still. Elizabeth made her way to her decrepit VW Bug and unlocked it. She opened the door, but didn't get in. She paused and lifted her head as if she'd heard something. Simon felt his heart lurch. He strained to see the threat, ready to go to her. After a painfully long moment, she shook her head and got into the car.

Simon let out a breath he didn't know he'd been holding and watched her pull out of the lot. He stood at the window long after the red of her tail lights had been swallowed by the night. What was it about that woman that left him feeling so undone? He was a solitary man, by choice and by circumstance. He'd grown used to living according to his own whim and no one else's. Then Elizabeth West had come into his life. She was curious, honest, unafraid and completely maddening. He had managed perfectly well without her and yet, he couldn't quite remember how.

18511923R00139

Made in the USA
Lexington, KY
09 November 2012